D1443189

Doing It at the Dixie Dew

This Large Print Book carries the
Seal of Approval of N.A.V.H.

Doing It at the Dixie Dew

Ruth Moose

THORNDIKE PRESS

A part of Gale, Cengage Learning

GALE
CENGAGE Learning®

Farmington Hills, Mich • San Francisco • New York • Waterville, Maine
Meriden, Conn • Mason, Ohio • Chicago

GALE
CENGAGE Learning®

LIBRARY OF CONGRESS CATALOGING-IN-PUBLICATION DATA

Moose, Ruth.
    Doing it at the Dixie Dew / by Ruth Moose. — Large print edition.
    pages ; cm. — (Thorndike Press large print mystery)
    ISBN 978-1-4104-7124-6 (hardcover) — ISBN 1-4104-7124-1 (hardcover)
    1. Women—Southern States—Fiction. 2. Bed and breakfast accommodations—Fiction. 3. Murder—Investigation—Fiction. 4. Large type books. I. Title.
    PS3563.O69D65 2014b
    813'.54—dc23   2014025670

Published in 2014 by arrangement with St. Martin's Press, LLC

Printed in Mexico
1 2 3 4 5 6 7 18 17 16 15 14

To Lyle, Robin, Jordan, Tyler and Barry,
Melissa, Mallorie, and Madison Moose,
with much love

CHAPTER ONE

People don't go to a bed-and-breakfast to die, do they? I'd never heard of it before, but let me tell you about Miss Lavinia Lovingood. She came to my bed-and-breakfast, the Dixie Dew, in Littleboro, North Carolina, checked in and "checked out." She died. Went to bed in my Azalea Room, fresh with deep pink paint and wallpaper still damp from the hanging, and never got up.

I couldn't believe it. There I was after my first night in the bed-and-breakfast business and I'd had six guests. Two couples and two singles. A full house. The two couples were a Mr. and Mrs. Elmer Ottinger from Hackensack and Will and Ann Dinsmore from Quebec. The singles, a Mr. Fred Fredricks from Forest Grove and a tiny ivory wisp of a woman, Miss Lavinia Lovingood, who was surely eighty plus but extremely well kept, if you know what I mean. She'd written for a room weeks ago, even before I knew I'd have a room ready. She'd written in perfect cursive on thick, monogrammed notepaper and enclosed a generous deposit for a three-night stay.

When the reservation came, Ida Plum Duckett, "my good right arm" and lifesaver in general, peeked over my shoulder and said, "Come home to die, did she?"

"Who?" I asked, wondering how somebody in Rome, Italy (not Rome, Georgia — around here you had to specify), knew about the Dixie Dew Bed-and-Breakfast. "You know her?"

"Beth Mckenzie Henry, if you knew anybody in this town, you knew a Lovingood," Ida Plum said. "Took the whole hill in the cemetery for themselves until they daughtered out. I guess she's the last one."

"Imagine," I said. "Somebody from Littleboro, North Carolina, living in Italy." I tapped my teeth with the envelope that smelled almost good enough to eat. A smell that had a hint of citrus and some delicate, delicious spice.

Ida Plum went back to folding the sheet she'd just ironed.

I've always thought, next to baking smells, the smell of clean, sun-dried laundry had to be right up there with the best in the world. I'd gone to sleep most of my childhood to the *whump, whump* of my grandmother ironing tablecloths for some wedding reception or anniversary party she was catering.

"Lavinia Lovingood must be eighty if she's a day," Ida Plum said. "Grew up in that mansion near the courthouse. Married some somebody from overseas, I heard tell, went to live abroad, and nobody's seen her since. Her mama and daddy died in a train wreck when she was eighteen or twenty and left her a bundle. In fact, a whole bunch of bundles. More bundles than anybody could count is what I always heard." Ida Plum stacked another finished sheet beside the ironer.

I remembered when my grandmother won that ironer in some sort of giveaway at the Western Auto Store on Main Street. I'd been eight or so at the time, and when they called to tell Mama Alice she'd won she just whooped, hugged me tight and whirled me around the kitchen. "Honeybunch," she said, "somebody up there really does like us. Maybe just a little."

When the *Littleboro Messenger,* which everybody around here calls *The Mess,* ran her picture on the front page under the heading "Local Native Wins" we laughed until our sides ached. For years after we called it "loco native" every time the newspaper used the term. "Local Native Graduates with Honors" or "Local Native Chosen First in This and That." Local native Margaret Alice McKenzie used that ironer to iron enough tablecloths and napkins to clothe the whole town and then some. Her catering business kept us both in jeans and sneakers, fed us and even sent me to art school in "that godforsaken Yankee land" (as my grandmother called Rhode Island). She never understood why I couldn't go someplace sensible like Atlanta. Or Florida. "Someplace warm," she always said when we packed my clothes each fall. "You'd save enough on wool sweaters to pay your tuition."

That April morning rain dripped from the eaves in crystal sheets. The house needed gutters . . . bad. The old ones, rusted to shreds and hanging on out of habit, had been taken down and hauled off when I had the new roof put on. A new roof paid for with a bank loan bigger than the national debt . . . or at least that's what it felt like to me.

I'd borrowed on the house, one of those big old barns with a wraparound porch on three sides, and the McKenzie good name. My grandmother believed in paying bills almost the same day she received them. Not owing anybody. And she believed in keeping things in good repair. A stitch in time and all that stuff. That's why I couldn't understand how she'd let the house "go."

When I came home last spring, I couldn't believe this was the same house I'd grown up in. It seemed to have fallen into disrepair overnight, peeling paint, rotten roof, rusted gutters. This was a house that had to be kept painted sparkling white, and every board seemed to slurp paint by the gallon. The painters I hired first thing after I got the loan kept buying paint and more paint, shaking their heads as they opened and stirred bucket after bucket. And I kept asking myself how it all seemed to have happened overnight. Like it had with her.

One day my grandmother was baking for a wedding reception for a hundred and fifty; the next she lay crumpled in a heap at the bottom of the basement stairs, unconscious. A state she stayed in for six months in The Oaks Nursing and Rest Home. Their motto was "You Rest with the Best." And Mama Alice *had* rested in the best of care. The kind that cleaned out her life savings and would have started on mine if I had any. The house would have gone next.

As it was, that was all I had left. Turning it into a bed-and-breakfast seemed to be about the only thing I could do with the "white elephant." It wasn't even in any condition to sell, take what I could get, get it off my hands and run, which had been one of my options. Run where? That had been my question, so I backed up and borrowed to the hilt and now I was sweating it out.

That was when Ida Plum Duckett showed up at my front door. In Littleboro you never had to run a classified ad for anything you needed. All you had to do was mention what you needed to anybody within earshot of anybody else and somebody would be on your porch within a week saying, "Heard tell you got a tree that needs downing." Or, "Heard tell you got plumbing troubles."

Ida Plum stood on my front porch that December day in her purple plaid coat and gray lace-up shoes, white crocheted beret and matching scarf. "Heard tell you're trying to turn this old barn into some fancy-schmancy bed-and-breakfast thing," she said.

I explained I wasn't in the position to hire anybody yet. Hadn't even started inside. Opening was months and mucho dollars down the road that sure wasn't paved with gold. Littleboro's not the kind of place for tourist trade. Just a dot on a lot of maps and bypassed off the Interstate. I wasn't likely to make a fortune. Just a small living was all I wanted. In a quiet town where everybody knew everybody's troubles *and* failings and forgave them.

Ida Plum said she was tired of sitting home gathering dust. She'd helped Mama Alice after I left for art school and stayed gone fifteen years. "Deserter," Mama Alice would tease when I called or came home summers and holidays. "I'm surprised you don't get stopped at the Mason-Dixon Line." She knew why I stayed in New England, in Maine, though she never met him. At least I never married him. I can say that for myself.

Sherman, my black-and-white cat who had been sitting beside the front door washing a paw and looking as if he knew a secret, shot in when I opened the door. Ida Plum followed. Cat and woman marched over that threshold, chins tilted toward the ceiling like they owned the place.

"But . . ." I started, and before I finished the sentence Ida Plum had hung her coat on the hall tree, taken off her beret and fluffed her hair.

"Money doesn't buy everything," she said. "I won't charge you what I'm worth. You couldn't afford me." She laughed. "Let's

13

just say I'm doing this as a favor for Margaret Alice." She named an hourly figure that I quickly shook on before she could change her mind.

That was how she came to man the ironer while I polished silver and waited for Miss Lavinia Lovingood to decide to descend the stairs and come to breakfast. "Surely she doesn't think she'll get breakfast in bed," I said to Ida Plum. It was nearly noon and everybody else had gone long ago. The Ottingers, who had the Periwinkle Room, left at seven, tiptoeing downstairs and taking their coffee and pecan muffins to go. The Dinsmores were through breakfast and gone by eight and Mr. Fredricks had two eggs over lightly, bacon, three cups of coffee, five muffins with fig preserves and apricot marmalade and waddled out the door before eight thirty. Only Miss Lavinia still slept.

I emptied stale coffee from Mama Alice's silver urn, rinsed and wiped off the water spots. I'd polished her assorted silver trays, large and small, legged and not, tea service, punch bowl, cups, ladles and serving pieces, candlesticks and flatware. My grandmother had a lot of old silver. Some she'd bought at antique shops and estate sales and some she'd gotten with Green Stamps. I remem-

14

bered sitting at the kitchen table licking and sticking stamps, counting the books until we had enough for this piece or that. Some of the silver had belonged to my mother, who selected the same pattern as Mama Alice. In the South, if a girl was smart she chose the same swirl of roses and ivy as her mother and someday she'd end up with service for twenty-four or thirty-six. Silver was my grandmother's way of investing. And my inheritance, along with the house. Except the silver was in better shape. Even on a drab day it gave off a soft glow.

Ida Plum fed another pink sheet into the soft, padded lips of the ironer. "Pity the poor man who sees these sheets on his bed and thinks he's got the wrong kind of house." She snorted a laugh through her nose.

"I'll send you up," I said, and measured out beans to grind to make more coffee, this time in a smaller pot. "I'll get you a long, blond wig and shove you up the stairs."

"He'd jump out the window when I came in the door." Ida Plum laughed. "My sex life died the day they carried Turner Duckett out the door, thank God. It never was much and I had enough to do without it."

I knew Ida Plum had one daughter who'd

gone straight from some women's college in the Midwest to California and didn't come back to Littleboro. Ever. Ida Plum visited her but didn't stay long. She said she could never live in a place where they *dried* okra and *arranged* it instead of breading and frying it. "Pure foolishness. Some people don't know good eating when it's put before them."

"Maybe she's one of those toast-and-tea people," I said, thinking of Miss Lavinia, and mentally chided myself for not asking when she checked in. I was learning.

"Pepto-Bismol," Ida Plum said, folding another freshly ironed sheet into a neat pink package. "That's the color of these sheets."

"I'm going to overlook that remark," I teased, and emptied the coffee into the percolator. "At my stage of the game, I can't afford to look sale horses in the mouth."

"PB pink is still PB pink in my book."

"Look at them this way," I said. "Those sheets are four-eighty-count, pima cotton. They don't have rosebuds or poppies or apples or cherries and they were cheap. El cheapo. Bargain with a great big *B*." Besides, I'd bought two dozen of them. Some for the beds and some to make tablecloths for the sunporch, which I was going to turn into a tearoom. Something Mama Alice

16

always talked about but never did. Who in Littleboro would come to tea? There was a book club or two and there had always been the Littleboro Women's Club and Junior Women's Club, but most of those met only once a month. Bridge groups? Lions Club? Somehow I couldn't see many men eating at a table covered in pink pima cotton.

"Think I ought to go tap on Miss Lavinia's door? See if she's all right?" I headed down the hall and had my hand on the newel post when I saw a shadow through the leaded-glass front door. Black. A man wearing black: black suit, black shirt and a white clerical collar. Below it swung a large silver cross on a chain. Father Joe Roderick. "What a bod," I said to Mama Alice the first time I saw him. "He's too good-looking to be a priest. It's a shame the church got him first. What a waste."

Father Roderick had reddish hair and enough freckles for three faces. He also had the firm and ready handshake of someone going to go fast and far in church circles. "Joe Roderick," he said when I opened the door. "St. Ann's."

As if I didn't know. St. Ann's was the smallest church in town and the only Catholic one; blue stone, copper steeple, it sat on the corner of Main and Second. I went

17

with Mama Alice when I was home, which wasn't often or much. The congregation had been the same handful, with a wide gap between those in blue jeans and T-shirts and the older, more moneyed members in suits and ties, the women in pastel crepe dresses overlaid with chunky gold jewelry. The real kind. Miss Tempie Merritt still tortured the asthmatic old organ. She tormented it like she whacked the fingers of her piano pupils. I wondered if she wiped off the organ keys with alcohol after each service like she did her piano at home when each pupil left. Weird woman. I'd known her all my life and she was just plain weird. The really weird thing was, as badly as she played, she kept on playing year after year after year.

Before today I'd seen Father Joe in tennis whites much more often than his working black. He played tennis on the high school courts and cut across the track field and several vacant lots to Main. "That charm and those legs will get him places with the church and all the blue-haired ladies in this town who clip coupons and sit on their CDs," I said to Mama Alice. "He'll honey talk them into leaving every cent they've saved to the church. All he has to do is smile those sparkling whites and hug them often and they'll melt millions." I wasn't worried about Mama Alice. Somehow she never seemed to get old and she certainly was no fool. Especially where money was concerned. She'd had to work too hard for what little she had. Sometimes she and I had sat in the front porch swing and watched Father Roderick dash home in time to change. He probably ended up saying Mass still damp from his shower.

Now Father Roderick, looking slightly damp from the April drizzle, stood on my front porch and handed me a gray suede handbag. "Beth, I think this belongs to your guest Miss Lovingood."

I must have looked puzzled.

"Miss Lavinia had tea with me yesterday and forgot her handbag. My housekeeper only found it this morning cleaning my study. Would you be kind enough to give it to her with my apologies for not returning it sooner?"

"I'd be glad to," I said, though I was sure she had not been concerned enough to let it disturb her sleep. It did give me an excuse to knock on her door. I watched Father Joe Roderick walk away. I thought, What's a good-looking guy doing at such a going-nowhere little church?

When Miss Lavinia checked in yesterday I thought she looked exactly like her handwriting. That precise cursive. Of the old school, Mama Alice would have said, when cursive was as important as needlework and tatting, who you married, where you went and who you were seen with. Miss Lavinia wore a gray suit of some soft leather that almost glowed, a lace blouse, gloves, stockings and the most beautiful, gleaming gray shoes.

"I'm Lavinia," she said, and extended her hand. "You must be Alice's granddaughter Beth. I do hope my room is ready." She signed the guest book, still wearing the largest, darkest sunglasses I'd ever seen. Bigger than those Jackie O. used to sport.

I took the pen and led Miss Lavinia upstairs. She climbed the stairs slowly, delicately, her hand barely resting on the rail as she went. She's like an aged movie star, I thought, someone very well kept, marvelously preserved, but fragile as the thinnest crystal.

At the top of the stairs Miss Lavinia nodded like I was about to be dismissed and said, "I've had a difficult day." She drew in the corners of her pale mouth. "Not unpleasant. Just difficult."

"Let me know if I can do anything to make you more comfortable," I said.

She turned then and said she sometimes

had trouble sleeping and often got up during the night to read or write letters. "Don't be alarmed," she said, "if you see my light at some unusual hour or hear me moving about." She seemed almost amused to be explaining herself.

"Okay," I said now to Ida Plum as I geared up to go knock on Miss Lavania's door. "And I bet you anything her suit was made of eel skin. But it would take too many eels, wouldn't it?"

"You're asking me?" Ida Plum said. "I wouldn't know an eel if it bit me on the nose. All I know is if it cost a lot, and she's wearing it, that's probably what it is. She always had everything she wanted. Those Lovingoods lived like royalty even when they lived in Littleboro."

"That mansion," I said, remembering the wedding cake of a house that presided on the block behind the courthouse. For years it sat empty, never sold or rented. Miss Lavinia must have kept the taxes paid from wherever she was. Every year it fell down more and there were always the stories of how haunted it was and kids daring each other to go in, spend the night, et cetera. It finally got so covered with kudzu the garden clubs petitioned to have it torn down. That was about the time the county ran out of office space in the courthouse, bought the lot and built the annex, a redbrick building with skylights and a fountain in the court-yard that taxpayers still grumbled about being a waste.

"Do you know if she ever came back over the years?"

"She may have kept in touch with certain ones. I wasn't in that crowd. She's your grandmother's generation."

"Here I go," I said. "It's almost noon. Surely she won't be upset if I wake her now."

The upstairs hall was so quiet I even found myself tiptoeing though nobody was in the other three bedrooms.

I tapped lightly on the door and called, "Miss Lavinia!"

There wasn't a sound. Not even a soft snore or a little cough. Everything was too quiet.

Ida Plum came up the stairs, arms full of sheets for the linen closet. "Maybe she's hard of hearing. Did you knock hard enough?"

I knocked again, hard and loud. The old door thumped and rattled. My fist actually ached, I'd knocked so hard.

Still no answer. No sound of movement inside. Nothing.

I knocked, called, knocked again.

Ida Plum nudged me aside and inserted the master key from its nail in the linen closet.

Miss Lavinia wasn't in bed. The room seemed to be empty. I noticed the window was open and my new lace curtains getting damp from the blowing rain. I ran to close the window and almost tripped over Miss Lavinia. She lay in a twisted lump of pink satin between the bed and the white wicker desk, one arm under and one arm out, a piece of paper nearby. The bouquet of lilacs, white tulips and Mama Alice's parsley I'd used for greenery was overturned and scattered across the floor. Miss Lavinia's satin slippers stood beside the bed and her matching robe lay across a chair. Her book and glasses were on the bedside table.

I touched her shoulder, a shoulder so cold I felt it through the fabric. "Oh." I pulled back.

Ida Plum reached around me, took Miss Lavinia's lace-covered wrist and felt for a pulse. "None," she said. "Better call nine-one-one. They'll get Eikenberry's."

The funeral home? Oh God, I thought, Oh . . . my . . . God.

"The phone." Ida Plum put both hands on my shoulders, turned me around and marched me from the room, aimed me toward the stairs. Then she closed Miss Lavinia's bedroom door, locked it tight, but not before I'd grabbed the piece of paper off the floor and shoved it in my pocket. I had even started to pick up the flowers before Ida Plum pulled me away. Some things you just do without thinking. It's like automatic pilot takes over. Then someone reminds you where you are and what has happened.

In the end, Ida Plum was the one to call 9ll. I stood in the kitchen shivering like a New England winter.

I pulled the paper from my pocket and read two words scribbled in Miss Lavinia's handwriting scrawled haphazardly across the page. "That is . . ." That is what? I asked. What?

I heard the MedAlert leave the fire station, wailing. The wailing got closer and louder and my grandmother's expression "loud enough to wake the dead" kept playing in my mind.

Except nothing would ever wake Miss Lavinia again.

CHAPTER TWO

"This town loves a funeral," I said. In the years I'd been away I'd forgotten exactly how much a funeral was an occasion in Littleboro. The funeral home, where the "viewing" took place, was a social gathering and the line of cars down Main Street was a status symbol. "Cars were parked clear down to the schoolhouse," or, "Honey, I stood in line for over an hour. I've never seen such a crowd," people said at the beauty shop and grocery store. Somehow I couldn't quite see that sort of picture for Miss Lavinia Lovingood. It was hard to imagine who would be at her viewing or funeral.

My grandmother, Margaret Alice Mc-Kenzie, who raised me, used to say this town went all out for a funeral. Every weekend come pouring rain, blasting sunshine or icy-fingered sleet, there's somebody out on the bypass selling artificial funeral wreaths. Wreaths with every color flower nature never made and ribbons that accuse or get to your guilt with sayings like "Remember Mama" or "Daddy, Gone but Not Forgotten" or "We Love You, Grandpa." I try to look the other way as I drive by, though there's not a ribbon that spells out my sins or advertises my guilt. Not one "Welcome Home, Prodigal Daughter" in the bunch.

Ida Plum laid a stack of sheets on the kitchen counter, cotton sheets, line dried, ironed. They smelled smooth and old-fashioned and as if somebody cared, a sweet-smelling bed. Had Miss Lavinia even noticed? Had it been a quick death? I felt a little chill remembering and wrapped my arms around myself.

"Would you look at all the cakes?" Scott stood at my kitchen table. "There's six layer cakes and two pound cakes." He counted like a child eyeing a picnic. Scott had become, by default, my contractor/go-to guy/general-knowledge person about restoring an ailing house. He had come to my rescue just as I was about to give up, give in and go. Go where? Anywhere but here.

When I first started on the Dixie Dew, I'd hired Jake Renfroe, somebody Verna Crowell from next door had said was "good."

Later I remembered Verna Crowell had said this with a giggle and her hand half over her mouth. Good at what? I should have asked her. Good at sending me faster toward rack and ruin?

Jake Renfroe would order materials that piled up on my porch and then not show up to do anything with them. Meanwhile, bills kept coming in for all he'd charged in my name. Finally I picked up the phone and fired him. He'd cried. It's hard to hear an old man blubber over the phone, but I held firm.

Then Ida Plum said call Scott Smith. I did. He came and we'd been working together ever since.

Now Scott stood here in my kitchen eyeing the cakes under various wraps and foils as if they were trophies. Verna rang the back bell at six this morning, carrot cake in hand. "I'm so sorry to hear about Lavinia. Such a loss," she said.

Verna lived in two rooms in a fifteen-room house that decayed more every day. Her house was a few years older than Mama Alice's and until the last ten years had been kept freshly painted and in good repair. The Crowells had money, but Verna wasn't about to spend it on heat in the winter or air-conditioning in the summer or paint and

27

plaster and repairs. She was probably one of those "little old ladies" whom Father Roderick's charm was wooing out of all they had.

I didn't know what to say. I'd never met Miss Lavinia Lovingood before she decided to come to this house and die. Miss Lovingood had looked so awful when Ida Plum and I found her, all doubled over, her hair in a tangle and her face frozen in such agony. And so cold. I got goose bumps every time I thought about it.

"Lavinia Lovingood and I were girls together," Verna said, then added before I could begin to count, "even if she was a good deal older. Of course we hadn't kept in touch. Not for years. Not until she wrote me."

"Wrote you?"

"About a month ago." Verna reached down and pinched off a dead tulip bloom. "You keep a bulb groomed and they'll last longer."

"I don't understand." I felt like putting out my hand to stop any more tulip molesting.

"Wrote she'd be in Littleboro three days and come by to see me. Said we'd talk old times, catch up on our lives." Verna turned, started across the porch. "Now look what

28

it's come to. But that's what we all come down to in the end, isn't it?"

I didn't know any answers except to extend the cake back in Verna's direction. "Please," I said. "You keep it."

But Verna insisted. "Beth, honey, you don't know when you'll need it. At times like this you just don't know what you'll need." She patted my hand with her soft, old, wrinkled, spotted one. "After all, what are neighbors for, if not at a time like this?" A dark, hairy mole on Verna's cheek wiggled when she smiled. I'd seen that mole all my life, wondered why it never got any bigger. When I was little, I thought it looked for all the world like a bug and would crawl off any minute.

Lord," I said after Verna left. "Word spreads fast. Around here all you have to do is whisper and it's all over town."

"Who could miss it?" Ida Plum stacked sheets in the linen closet. "It's hard not to notice an ambulance backed up to a house, a body being hauled out in broad daylight."

Miss Lavinia had looked so natural. Just old, eighty plus, maybe heading hard toward ninety. People die in their sleep, I told myself. She just happened to be a guest and sleeping in my house when it happened.

"That's the way I want to go," Florence

Carelock said when she came to the back door with her Lemon Creme Delight Cake. "It's such a peaceful thing. Of course we don't get to choose, but if we could, that's what I'd want."

I tried to give back the cake.

"I have been your grandmother's friend all these years," she said, "and I want to do this much to help you out."

If you want to help me out, I thought, you'd let me forget this ever happened in my house. You'd help me get clean linens on some beds, vacuuming done and guests welcomed and checked in. But I only smiled and thanked Florence.

Four cakes came in after that. Delmore Simpson brought a pound cake, and the preacher, John Pittman from the Presbyterian church, brought another. His wife always kept a cake in the freezer for such emergencies, he said, and her name was already taped to the bottom of the plate, though there was no hurry getting the plate back.

It's not an emergency, I wanted to say. By this time, though, I'd learned to accept these food gifts and be grateful. Plus gracious. That was the least I could be. People meant well, I supposed. But in the back of my mind, I also wondered how much was simply curiosity and a cake was a ticket in the door.

"I wanted to go over some of the plans with you," Pastor Pittman said.

"Me?" I said. "What plans?"

"The funeral services for Lavinia Lovingood are to be at First Church and I thought Thursday would be a better day to do it than Friday. We're not supposed to have rain and I already have a golf date that morning and a wedding at four in the afternoon. Of course we don't want to wait until Saturday or Sunday . . . that's much too long, I think, don't you?"

"For who?" I said, though of course I knew. Miss Lavinia. But who decided these things? Surely she had family somewhere. Cousins? Nieces, nephews? Somebody? A life she left for a few days that had now become a life she left forever.

"All her family is in Littleboro Cemetery. There was so little of it really. She's the last, I suppose." He penciled in his appointment book. "Two o'clock suit you? We could make it three?"

"I didn't know her," I said.

"But of course you want to be at her services," Pastor Pittman said. "After all, she passed in this house . . . your house, your grandmother's house."

31

"That was an accident," I said.

"Sad, but it can be expected," Pastor Pittman said. "The Lovingoods were one of the founding families, foremost families, if I might call them that, of Littleboro. You ought to read our church history. Lavinia was the only child, the last of the Lovingoods, and she'd been away from this town over fifty years." He looked sweetly at me, gave a strained, patient smile. "Why, her family gave four of the eight stained-glass windows in our church . . . surely you've noticed. The Herringfield Windows."

Herringfields? Lovingoods? I thought. Where did they fit together?

"The wife's family," Pastor Pittman said. "They were the wealthy ones originally, and all the windows were given in old Mrs. Lovingood's maiden name."

Pittman was the pastor at First Presbyterian, but Miss Lavinia had been having tea with Father Roderick at St. Ann's. Why? Had she converted when she lived in Italy? I could see that. Maybe she even saw the Vatican every time she looked out her window. Maybe she even had tea with the Pope on occasion. Who knows? I guess now we'd never know.

"Oh." I remembered the stained-glass windows at church, two on each side of the pulpit. I'd spent a lot of Sunday mornings of my life until I went away to art school staring at *Jesus in the Garden,* his red flowing robe; *Jesus in the Temple* with the cat-o'-nine tails; Jesus suffering the little children (Mama Alice explained the scriptures on that one for years) and Jesus with the woman at the well.

Mama Alice had been a lapsed Catholic and First Presbyterian had the best youth group, so I went to both churches. Early Mass at St. Ann's, then regular service at First Church so I could go to Youth Group that night and on Wednesdays. It was the only social life for teens in Littleboro. My friend Malinda had done the same except she and her mom, Rosalie, had been pillars of St. Ann's.

"One always wants to come home, doesn't one?" Pittman said. A slight smile played at a corner of his mouth. He drummed his appointment book. "No matter how far one goes, home is still the place you want to come back to."

He left through the front door and admired the leaded fanlight as he went. "You're doing wonders with this old house," he said. "Paint really perks things up." Paint and the sweat putting it on, I wanted to say, plus what it cost. "I think it would have been cheaper to just cover it with money . . . paste on bills like wallpaper," Ida Plum said once.

I closed the door. Mama Alice always kept the glass door panels curtained, but I liked them bare, more light in the gloomy hall, on that dark curving staircase. Sunday evening Lavinia Lovingood had gone up those stairs alive, Monday afternoon she had been carried down dead. I turned quickly toward the kitchen where Scott and Ida Plum sat eating cake. "This Lemon Creme is heaven on a plate," he said. "There ought to be a law against doing something this good with food." He sliced another piece, slid extra icing off the knife with his finger, then licked his finger, closed his eyes and smiled.

"So what do I do with the rest of them?" I asked.

"How are you fixed for freezer space?" Ida Plum asked. "You could be in the tearoom business tomorrow." Ida Plum was on my side. Bless her. By converting the glassed-in side porch into a usable space, I would not only provide breakfast-eating space for the overnight guests but also be able to serve light lunches and snacks. The tearoom would provide extra income . . . after it got started and business built up. Mama Alice had been known as the best cook in Little-boro. She catered weddings, bridesmaids' luncheons and monthly meals for various civic clubs in town. In addition to the house, she'd left me a treasured hoard of tried and truly great recipes.

"This funeral business," Scott said. "I'm surprised Ed Eikenberry didn't put a wreath of white flowers on the door and some signs out front. He loves to advertise. In fact, I've never seen anybody enjoy the way they make their living quite as much as Ed Eiken-berry."

"Oh, he wanted to," Ida Plum said. "I stopped him."

"Thank God," I said. "That's all I need to greet arriving guests. Word would spread fast in the B-and-B business. 'Come to the Dixie Dew and Die,' or 'At the Dixie Dew They Do You In.' Can't you just see it? 'At the Dixie Dew We Specialize in Resting in Peace.' "

"You could add an 'R.I.P.' on your logo," Scott said. "Or 'For Your Final Rest, Dixie Dew Is the Best.' " He drew a banner in the air with his hands.

Ida Plum hooted from the hall, then went upstairs.

I laughed and laughed until my cheeks burned and my eyes watered. "Stop, stop.

It's not funny. It's awful."

"You're right," Scott said. He put his plate in the dishwasher. "But don't let the ghosts get to you. The Guilt Ghosts. None of it's your fault. It could happen to anyone, anywhere, anytime. The Dixie Dew and you weren't singled out as a spot on the map for Miss Lavinia's demise." He wrapped cakes for the freezer, put his name on the label of the chocolate pound cake and drew a skull and crossbones underneath.

"Scott!" I said.

"Don't get rattled. That's just to ensure this baby is mine. In case anybody robs freezers."

"Nobody robs freezers. Or if they do, they take roasts and steaks. Not chocolate cakes."

"Insurance," he said, and started to the basement to Mama Alice's freezers. The freezers were two oversized commercial units that stood side by side like giant white coffins. Mama Alice bought them when a restaurant in Raleigh went out of business. She got them for a song, she always said, and in the catering business she said they saved her life. She baked weeks ahead for a party or wedding reception.

Ida Plum had gone upstairs to vacuum. The door to Miss Lavinia's room was sealed and would be left that way for a while; even the bed was not to be changed. Police Chief Oswald DelGardo had sent his best and brightest, Bruce Bechner, over with the crime scene tape Monday night. Bruce bustled about like he was sealing off a presidential suite. That still left plenty to do, and who knew what tonight would bring? I didn't want to think about it. One dead guest in my bed-and-breakfast had been one too many.

"Honest," I said. "It wouldn't help business if word got out in the trade. Three days in business, I'm trying to get listed in the guidebooks and registers, approved by the B-and-B national board, and zonk, I have a death on my hands."

"Forget it," Scott said as he put the pineapple cake in the refrigerator. He surprised me being so easy to work with in a kitchen, but then he lived alone (I assumed) and was used to the ways of a kitchen. He seemed at ease here, almost from the first day. Instead of bringing a thermos of coffee from home, he brought coffees, freshly ground cinnamon and mocha coffees, hazelnut, amaretto, rum and almond, and made them here.

"Since when did any grocery store in Littleboro go gourmet?" I asked.

"Who says I only shop in Littleboro?" He

poured me a cup of some exotic mixture that had perfumed the whole house as it perked. Coffee always smelled better than it tasted, I thought, but wouldn't say such a thing aloud for anything.

My hand touched his as I took the cup and I thought how warm his fingers were, how strong. Fingers that had taken this house and started pulling it into shape. Helping make it into a business. Warm hands and a sturdy, dependable presence that had too quickly become an everyday part of my life, which scared me a little. I took the coffee and turned away. You learned a lot of things through pain, and one of the things was not to get too close to whatever caused it. But Scott wasn't Ben Johnson and Scott was here when I needed him, at least for now.

Scott always said he came when I called him. That much was true. When I first came back to the Dixie Dew, he pulled his truck into my driveway, got out and strode, both hands in the pockets of his jeans, straight toward a stack of materials Jake Renfroe had ordered and not used. Scott walked around the tarp-covered stuff, inspected it as if it were a used car and he could hardly restrain himself from kicking the tires . . . if there had been any. He stepped onto the porch, introduced himself and shook my hand, then went back to his truck for a clipboard and tape measure.

I offered to show him around, but he said, "I'd rather poke around on my own for a while. Then I'll have better questions and save you time. I charge by the hour, but I'm not on your clock yet." He bent to check a loose board on the front porch, lifted it looking for termites, then poked the decay to test for dry rot. He didn't comment. I knew the house was solid. It just needed a million gallons of paint and a new roof and a heating and cooling system and a new kitchen and enough wallpaper to roll out a road to China and . . . the list was endless.

"Uh-huh," Ida Plum had said when I came in the kitchen. "You got a live one now."

"Who is he?" I asked. I thought Scott looked familiar, but I wasn't sure.

"You know him," Ida Plum said. "You've known him all your life."

"Me?" I asked. "Not really." The name rang a faint bell, but I think I'd remember that face, those eyes so blue they took your breath away, those dark curls. "He would be better looking if he didn't have that smart-aleck smile pasted on his face," I said.

"He married Cedora," Ida Plum said as

39

she rinsed a dish.

"Ohmygosh," I said. "Not the Hollywood Princess. Not Miss Broadway Bound. Not Miss Talent Running out Her Rear End."

"That one. Nobody ever understood it. Both sets of parents tried to have it annulled."

"So what then?"

"She went to Broadway and took him along."

"She went to Hollywood and he came home. I think I get the picture now," I said. Cedora Harris, who called herself Sunny Deye, could now be heard singing commercial jingles: dishwashing liquids, body soaps, floor mop stuff. You had to know her voice, that clear, distinctive, lovely voice, to know it was Cedora. I had been two years behind Cedora in school. Her presence was so strong it probably still had an aura in the halls of Littleboro High. She was like something God dropped in the wrong place. That red-gold hair, green eyes and a figure the boys fell over. Poor Scott.

When he found me later, I was on the sunporch scraping paint off one of a million windows. "Tearoom," I said. "The rest of the house will be a bed-and-breakfast and this will pick up some of the lunch trade, the garden clubs, bridge groups, that sort of thing."

"You an idealist?" he asked. "The world eats idealists for breakfast. I've been chewed up and spit back out a few times."

I felt like taking my paintbrush to his face, that smug, know-it-all, sardonic look. "Does that mean you're out? You won't take on this job?"

"It means I will, but on my own terms."

I waited, didn't look at him, just scraped paint as hard and fast as I could. I turned my back to him and scraped as if he had left, as if there were no one in the room but me and my life depended on getting off this old paint. Dry shards flew in my face, made me cough. I didn't have to hire him and it didn't cost me anything to listen.

"I've got a couple of good people I call on from time to time, but mostly I'll do a lot of the work myself," he said. "I'm versatile and I've restored a half dozen or so of these big boxes in a couple of the counties around here. I'll work it flextime. Which means I may come in early and leave late or come in late and leave early. I may work nights or Saturdays or Sundays or holidays or whenever I've got materials on hand and time. My time is by the hour and I'll show you a weekly running tab on where we are. Can you work with that?"

Could I refuse? It wasn't like a dozen stood in line bidding for the job. I'd hired Jake Renfroe and for two months all he'd done was order materials, smoke his pipe, go around knocking it against the walls and say, "Miss Bethie, your grandma was some fine lady." Sometimes I felt like going to Verna and just asking why the heck she had ever recommended Jake Renfroe to do the work. Was she trying to set me up for failure? If so, why? She and Mama Alice had been close as sisters. Or I thought they were.

There was nobody else in town to take on something like this. Littleboro was a do-it-yourself or do-without town. "You're on," I said.

He reached for my hand, which was covered with dust and paint flecks. I extended my hand and he took it. "You just hired the best," he said.

And certainly the most modest in the business, I wanted to add but didn't.

Scott had made the renovating a project, a challenge, a puzzle to solve. Like Miss Lavinia's death.

Surely Miss Lavinia had not been in any pain. Surely she would have cried out, called to me for help, tried to come downstairs. I hoped Miss Lavinia Lovingood died a simple, good and natural death. Even Ed Eikenberry said it looked that way, but he wouldn't know for sure until the autopsy came back from Chapel Hill. Probably Thursday or Friday. Meanwhile plans for her services were in progress, full swing.

Like Mama Alice always said, this town turned out for a funeral. And they surely did for my grandmother's six months ago. Police Chief Ossie DelGardo, the hearse, family cars, funeral procession, even if it was only five blocks from any church in town to Littleboro Cemetery. Bruce Beckner, his assistant (who was also the rest of the Littleboro Police Department), stood at the courthouse square, hat held over his chest, and stopped traffic for the funeral. Anyone from out of town would think it showed respect. How wonderful this remaining bit of Americana, this little town keeping a quaint custom long after big cities raced past and forgot it. Truth was, Ossie DelGardo and Bruce Beckner didn't have one earthly thing else to do but drive around in their respective cars and confer at Will's Bar-B-Que west of town, where the hickory logs were split and stacked tall as a fence behind it and the little pink pig's four neon feet never stopped running. Nor did the scented smoke stop permeating the town, sunup to sundown, six days a week.

Miss Lavinia had paid for three days. I would have to refund two days to her estate, wherever that was. Miss Lavinia, I wanted to say, wherever you are, couldn't you have waited until your three days were up, then gone somewhere else to do it?

Do it, I thought. That sounded like sex. In high school and college you were asked, "Did you do *it*?" And everyone knew which girls "did *it*," which couples were "doing *it*."

Miss Lavinia didn't do *it*. She died. And she didn't have any choice in the matter. Or did she? The real question was, why had she come back to Littleboro at all? And what the heck did those two little cryptic words on her note mean?

It was so strange. All of this. Strange and unsettling. Maybe coming back to Littleboro wasn't the right thing to do at this point in my life. Maybe all this was taking my life in some direction I didn't want to go.

CHAPTER THREE

I grabbed my old plaid windbreaker from the hook on the back porch and walked down Main Street to Littleboro Cemetery. Back at the house I knew the phone was ringing, people were in and out. Before I'd left, one guest called to cancel. I couldn't help but wonder if he really had a last-minute change of plans or if the news of Miss Lovingood's demise had already traveled two hundred miles. And if so, how much farther would it go? Bad news always wore winged shoes. And gossip danced with taps on its heels.

"Go," Ida Plum said. "You need some fresh air. I'll hold the fort. Mind the store. Tend the shop . . . whatever." She waved me away with her dust cloth. The vacuum cleaner stood behind her like a retired soldier, worn but still staunch. Mama Alice's stalwart old Hoover, its burgundy bag of a paunch faded as damask. Its motor sounded like gravel in a blender.

I walked down Main Street. Verna Crowell's lilac bushes were lit with lavender candles. I drew in the deep blue smell. The old lilacs were thick as a hedge behind Verna's wrought-iron fence, and the fence was so rusted and sprawled you had to know it was there to see it. Something moved behind the curtains at one of the windows. Verna? Or her darn rabbit, Robert Redford? Sometimes he hopped onto a chair and sat looking out, his red eyes like two tiny coals in the darkened rooms. Verna's old galleon of a house begged for paint, gallons and gallons and gallons of paint, and a team of ten men with ladders and buckets and brushes to apply it. Verna's house was even worse than Mama Alice's. If Scott Smith was smart he'd open up a paint store in this town and take food stamps in trade. Except people like Verna didn't get food stamps. They had money, probably lots of money, yet lived like street people once removed.

I'd walked to the cemetery a lot in the months I'd been back.

It had been six months since Mama Alice died, been buried next to Granddaddy McKenzie, who died when I was a week old. Beside their graves was my mother's, Alice

McKenzie Henry's. Mama had stepped off the curb in front of the courthouse straight into the path of a transfer truck. She was killed instantly. I was seven, in the second grade. Mama Alice had come for me, walked me home and been mother, grandmother and good friend until last year. Beside my mother's grave was a flat, empty space, marked and set aside for Andrew Buie Henry, who went to Vietnam and never came back. Missing in action. All my childhood, those words haunted me. I wanted to believe they meant my father was still alive, that Andrew Henry was more than a framed photograph on my dresser and a few scattered memories of a tall man with dark hair and a deep laugh. The grave was empty. That meant it waited for something or someone, as an empty space lay marked and waiting for Lavinia Lovingood, who'd come home to die. I hoped that she, herself, had come home to live, make a life for herself in Littleboro.

The Lovingood mausoleum was a solid cement little house on the hill in the back corner of Littleboro. It had been there all my life, and I never thought much about it. The name Lovingood never meant anything to me before either.

The mausoleum was big, impressive,

carved with pillars and scrolls, ornate columns. Tall cedars stood at each corner of a rusted iron fence. Several dogwood trees leaned near the two tombs, tombs impressive enough to encase Pharaohs.

The Lovingood section was only equaled in Littleboro by another heavily fenced family plot in the opposite corner which held the Merritt mausoleum. Inside the Merritts' fence, a woman in a faded yellow dress knelt over a grave.

I stopped, stood very still. I felt as if I'd been caught somewhere I wasn't supposed to be. My own family plot with Mama and Mama Alice was far down the hill, beyond the fountain, little benches, plantings and trees.

The woman at the Merritt mausoleum arranged a vase of brown plastic chrysanthemums on the ground at her feet and talked to herself. "I miss my sweetheart, my love, precious . . ." I started away, but my footsteps on the gravel startled the woman, who turned around. "Oh," she said. Both hands flew immediately to her cheeks. "Who's there? What do you want?"

"I'm sorry," I said. "I didn't mean to disturb you."

"I'm not used to anyone being in this cemetery," the woman said. She seemed calmer now, walked toward the fence and peered at me. "You're Alice McKenzie's girl, aren't you?" Her small eyes, black as onyx, were bright and piercing in her patchwork face of heavy rouge over extremely white skin and a thick stitching of wrinkles. "Miss Tempie?" I asked. I'd taken piano lessons from Tempie Merritt for a year when I was eight, came home crying with red fingers after each session. After the nightmares began, Mama Alice let me stop the lessons. The nightmares also stopped. I couldn't tell my grandmother then how Miss Tempie whacked my hands with a ruler for every wrong note, how the huge Merritt house two blocks over was always cold and smelled of rubbing alcohol. To this day the smell of rubbing alcohol made me gag. Tempie was deathly afraid of germs. And yet here she was still alive, more than twenty years later, germs and all. I wondered if she still taught? How many rulers she'd broken during her teaching career? Or how many little fingers and egos she had bruised and damaged? I wondered if today's parents knew and still accepted her "teaching methods."

Miss Tempie was even thinner than I remembered; her bones seemed almost sharp enough to puncture the faded cotton shirtwaist dress. And her soiled white sweater, crookedly buttoned, looked angled as a bent clothes hanger. She tried to smooth her hair, almost white now, with touches of the blond she used to be. She still wore her thin hair pulled back, pinned in an irregular and awkward roll, with wisps escaping around her head like a swarm of white moths.

"It's Harold," Miss Tempie whispered. She turned to look behind her. A large man in dark green work clothes and a bill cap stood beside Miss Tempie's old black Cadillac, a monster of a car so old its fenders, spots on the trunk and hood, looked as though they'd been polished through to the body paint. The man held a shovel. His bulk cast a thick shadow toward us.

"Harold?" I didn't know any Harolds. Certainly not a Harold Merritt. Miss Tempie didn't have a brother, nor a son that I knew about. Who was Harold?

"My poodle. I know you're not supposed to, but it was the family plot, and Harold was with us nineteen years. That's old for a poodle. I couldn't bury him just anywhere." Miss Tempie twisted her handkerchief with a tatted edge. Her fingers looked knotted and blue.

Oh God, I thought, that's what money

50

would do. The Merritts had owned this town along with the Lovingoods, only the Merritts lived longer, held on to their money and influence. Miss Tempie probably had slipped whoever gravedigger was in charge of the cemetery a twenty or two and together they smuggled dead Harold into the family plot. Nobody knew or cared, or if they did, they looked the other way. Miss Tempie turned back to the grave. "I didn't want to let him go," she said. Her voice quavered like a tired old mourning dove. "He slept at the foot of my bed every night. This last year . . . this last year, he couldn't climb up there by himself and I had to lift him. He weighed next to nothing toward the end. And then one morning he wasn't there. Not the real Harold, just his little fur suit." She bent to the ground weeping, crying, moaning.

"I'm so sorry," I said, and touched her shoulder. Sad to think all she had to love was a poodle. I thought Harold was probably the kind of poodle that humped all the kids' legs as they took piano lessons. I felt lucky to have escaped knowing him. Lucky I didn't have to go in that house, where the odor was so dark and thick I used to come out and take a dozen deep breaths to get the smell out of my lungs.

I couldn't go to the McKenzie family plot, though the spring grass on Mama Alice's grave would be bright and tender. Too much sorrow for me still.

I walked away as quietly as I could. All that wet and loud grief was getting to me. Miss Tempie had surely livened up my walk "to get away from it all." Until today the cemetery had been a fine and private place.

Still not ready to go home, I walked past the Dixie Dew, around the courthouse square, and headed for the library in the new big concrete box of the Government Complex. The whole thing was so cold and modern it made me think I was in another town. One without heart and soul and history. The old library, the one I'd grown up with, had been on the next block, a red-brick building that had mellowed almost brown over the years. Inside it was full of paneling, balconies and tall shelves you needed a rolling stepladder to reach. I loved it. I'd spent half my growing-up years reading in one of the wing chairs beside the green marble fireplace, or on rainy days gazing out the tall windows toward the courthouse and the statue of the Confederate soldier. In the winter I could see past it through the water oak trees along Main

Street to the blue roof of Mama Alice's house.

As soon as I stepped through the double glass doors, Ethelene Smart said, "Wasn't it just awful about Lavinia Lovingood?" Ethelene had been reference librarian in Littleboro for as long as I remembered. "That poor woman," she said, and laughed. "Not that you could call any of the Lovingoods poor." Ethelene wore her long brown hair, heavily streaked with gray, pulled back in a ponytail that switched and swayed when she moved. She had a pencil poked behind one ear. Her movements were brisk as a wren and she talked in a high chirrup of a voice. "Lord, those Lovingoods had money all the way back to King Midas. They were drinking tea out of little china cups when the rest of us around here were still using gourd dippers." She took me to a large brass wall plaque in the local history room that said it had been donated by the Lovingood family. Then Ethelene pulled a Littleboro Historical Society book off the shelf and pointed out a blurred photo of the old Lovingood house that had stood on this corner until the Government Complex was built. It looked as large and imposing in the photo as I remembered, white and ghostly, tall columns and wide porch.

A patron dinged the dinger at the checkout desk and Ethelene hurried over as fast as any spinster librarian in her sensible shoes could go.

I was too tired and distracted to read magazines; none of the new novels grabbed my attention and I didn't think I wanted to involve myself in a murder mystery. I'd read all the "cat" mysteries, and I didn't like those "fast city cop" or "macho men on houseboats" types.

I didn't go into the drugstore. Malinda was off on Wednesdays. She had probably taken her son, Elvis, to the park or fishing or to hang around a service station while her car was being greased and the oil changed. Malinda might be raising her child by herself, though she said her mother would get her feathers ruffled if anybody ever hinted at such a thing. Malinda did try to do a few macho things with her son. She quoted all kinds of statistics about black males to me: health and longevity and education and role models. Elvis wouldn't lack anything Malinda could give him, I thought, but a live-in father. You can grow up without one, but not without a lot of scars and questions and anger. I knew about that and sometimes I tried to lay all that blame in my past with Ben. You can't divorce someone you haven't been married to, but ending the relationship feels the same, leaves scars, too. So does life. No one gets through it without some physical and emotional scratches and mending. Funny though, Miss Lavinia, as old as she was, had looked so serene, so at peace with herself, when she had checked in at the Dixie Dew. I had been taken with her countenance; she was old, but she was regal and there was a glow about her. A glow that had gone overnight into a death pallor. It was hard for me to believe. On my way home, I skirted the old courthouse, its redbrick the same mellowed brown the old library had been. At least that building had not changed, just been outgrown, and since it stood on its own little island in the middle of town it couldn't be added on to. Hence the new Government Complex, built behind it and just a step away. The old courthouse was still in use, and in some little basement office a clerk filled out the death certificate on Lavinia Lovingood, age eighty-something, born Carelock County, died Carelock County. And somewhere in some small cubbyhole at *The Mess* I wondered if Fanny Upchurch was typing out Miss Lavinia's obituary.

Would they run it front page, not giving

her age, of course, but a couple paragraphs about the Lovingoods' being one of Littleboro's most prominent families, and so on? And a photo of Miss Lavinia from her debutante days? Or her college yearbook? Somehow I knew she was beautiful. I just hoped the obituary didn't include the information that she died in the Dixie Dew, recently renovated and now open as a B and B by local native Beth Henry.

Bruce Beckner from the police department had said, "Don't touch anything in this room." He had taken Miss Lavinia's handbag, looked through her wallet, credit cards, and flipped through her cash like the winner at a gaming table. "Ten thousand dollars." He whistled. "That's traveling." He fanned through the bills with the tips of his fingers.

They'd sealed off the room, just in case. "Until the lab reports are in," Bruce had said. Right now, for all I cared, they could seal off that room forever.

And they left Miss Lavinia's little car parked out front: some sort of cute little foreign-looking sporty convertible. Scott said having it parked out there didn't tear down the neighborhood a bit. It was locked and Ossie DelGardo would get around to moving it in a few days. Until then, it did grace the neighborhood with an elegant presence, though a glance at it did send a chill of something ominous down the back of my neck.

Before Bruce came with his handy-dandy roll of crime scene tape, Ida Plum had gone into Miss Lavinia's room and pulled the eel-skin suit and the lace blouse off the hangers. Then Ida had gone into Miss Lavinia's drawers and gotten a slip, bra and panties, stockings and shoes. "I think she'd want to be buried well," Ida Plum said, smoothing across her arm the most beautiful underwear I'd ever seen. "Handmade," she sighed. "I'll drop them by Eikenberry's on my way home." Trust Ida Plum to think of such things, the finishing touches.

I felt like the whole thing with Miss Lavinia was so strange, so unreal. Walking helped me get my feet back on the ground.

I turned the corner at the courthouse and remembered twenty years or so ago there had been talk about tearing the old court-house down. Thank goodness some county commissioner or historic-minded group had opposed it. A sleek black marble glass box would stick out in this town like a pyramid. Besides, I snickered, they'd have to move the statue of the Confederate soldier. I could see him from my bedroom window.

Always on guard, his rifle pointed to the sky, as I slept, protected. Had he been Miss Lavinia's last look, that stone statue through the trees holding up the sky? A little halt in time? She'd been as close to home as she could get. I was glad about that. Littleboro had been able to give her something, and the sight of Mama Alice's house being restored must have been a small comfort. Even when the rest of the town whispered loudly I'd never make it a successful bed-and-breakfast.

I stepped past a stack of cement bags. Behind it lay lumber, scaffolding. The Redfern house had been torn down, a façade of Southern homes built in its place. Condominiums. Ida Plum had said the Catholic diocese was building those. Seven units followed the façade like cars on a train. Who would buy those? How many people had moved to Littleboro last year? Three? Probably those three were not looking for two-hundred-eighty-thousand-dollar condominiums, but somebody might think big, bigger than I, and they'd have either more money or better credit or know something I didn't know.

As I opened my own gate, I saw the swing of something orange-red on the lower limbs of the huge water oak in front of the town's water tower. Crazy Reba was back in town. Oh Lord, she'd probably be at the funeral tomorrow. Not knowing where she was, dressed in parts of five different outfits and singing nursery rhymes. That was sad, too. Crazy Reba had been plain Reba Satterfield in high school. A little loud and strange, but she'd graduated with the rest of them. Married somebody, had five kids in four years, and her mind kicked out. She was one of the revolving-door cases for the courts and hospitals for the mentally ill. Not considered a danger to herself or others, she lived on the streets and under the tree, hanging her clothes across the limbs, sleeping on and under them at night. Mama Alice had fed her, given her blankets, only to find in the morning that Reba had used the blankets to drape Mama Alice's boxwoods. Reba never slept inside. She said she didn't like walls. Sad, I thought again, and the sadness seemed like a gray cloud following me home.

On my own walk, I meandered, checked Mama Alice's boxwoods for spider mites, noted the grass needed mowing. There was an apron of a yard on each side of the walk, usually mowed with the push mower Mama Alice had used until last year. Mama Alice must have known Miss Lavinia, I thought.

Maybe she would have known why Lavinia Lovingood had come back, but Mama Alice was dead. For a moment I ached for those arms I'd always gone to for answers and comfort.

Ida Plum met me in the kitchen. She waved the wand to the vacuum cleaner like a dark warning flag. "Don't go upstairs," she said. "They've dusted for prints. Miss Lavinia was murdered."

Well hell, I thought, that's just what Ossie DelGardo wants. To turn Littleboro into some big-city crime scene. Oh, he is in his glory, but I didn't believe it for a minute. There had to be a glitch somewhere. At least I hoped there was.

CHAPTER FOUR

Thursday morning I watched a silver curtain of rain slide off the roof. Yesterday seemed like a blur. Three guests for the Dixie Dew. In, out. I hardly saw them. In fact, the whole week had been very blurred, very fuzzy and not the way I liked my life to be. I wanted a crisp, clean, organized, smoothly clicking along kind of life. Not one that kept falling apart and I had to pick up the pieces, salvage what I could and start all over again. My life lately had been like this house, badly in need of care and attention.

Oh, this house needs gutters, I thought, beautiful long, new gleaming gutters and downspouts that cost like the dickens, and right now I couldn't take out another loan for them. Not until I'd hacked my way heavily at the present one. That was my first thought. My second thought was Miss Lavinia. It was pouring rain on the day of her funeral, and it looked and sounded like one of those rains that would go on steadily throughout the day and continue into the night. Poor Miss Lavinia.

I unplugged my warming tray in the dining room that kept muffins, Danish and bacon ready to serve and started upstairs, where Ida Plum had taken off the dirty linens. I started to vacuum the Periwinkle Room. I walked quickly by the tightly shut and sealed door to the Azalea Room, tried not to think, just started laying out fresh towels, smoothing on clean linens, working steadily, mindlessly, in the Lobelia Room.

I found burgundy leather slippers had been left under the bed. Mr. Holtzman. I'd have to write him, see if he wanted them sent. And Mrs. Frick, in the Green Room, had left a package of tights in the bathroom . . . I assumed they were hers and didn't belong to either Mr. Holtzman or Mr. Frick. There was a gold earring under the dresser. I bagged and labeled them for the basket under the lobby desk. I'd have to write Mrs. F. also.

I bumped into Ida Plum with the cleaning cart, took supplies and started on the bathroom. Then I buffed the hardwood floors Scott and I had sanded, rubbed to a gleam with wax and stain. They were the charm of the second floor. Guests loved them. And the cute area rugs in front of the fireplaces and beside the beds. Scott and I had bought the rugs at an auction, cleaned, aired and sunned them. The effect was cozy, but cozy wouldn't warm anyone this winter. The cold truth was really cold. Unless I put in a new furnace, the upstairs was going to be rented by only the most hardy. Scott had the idea of offering guests an electric blanket, a space heater for the bathroom, and in the morning presenting them with an endurance certificate. I didn't think we'd get many takers, except possibly some sturdy stalwarts. Though I'd grown up that way and it hadn't hurt me a bit. In fact, being used to cold rooms had been a boon for me those Maine winters.

I dusted and decided these rooms wouldn't get fresh flowers from the back garden unless the rain stopped. And Miss Lavinia wouldn't get many mourners. How could she have when she'd been gone from Littleboro so long? No children, no siblings. No cousins? Maybe somewhere there was a first cousin or a first cousin once removed.

"Except Elsie Shimpock," I said aloud.

"What?" Ida Plum asked as she wound the cord on the vacuum.

"Elsie Shimpock, the town mourner. Is she still alive? She may be the only one at

Miss Lavinia's funeral. That's all she used to do, go to funerals, whether she knew the person or not. She went, and she wept. Beautifully."

"You think she'll show up for Miss Lavinia?" Ida Plum said. She took her dustcloth, polished the stair rail. "Does the sun rise? Is water wet?"

"She'll show up like a prop. She'll be there in black. Hat, umbrella, all." I almost laughed. "Mama Alice said if Elsie Shimpock showed up at her funeral, I was to shoot her."

"Did she?" Scott asked as he came up the stairs. "And most importantly, did you?" Scott wore a blue-checked shirt and jeans. God, he looked good in jeans, I thought, then looked away.

"Shoot her? Of course not, but I honestly don't remember seeing her there. She's creepy."

"And you, Ida Banana? You going?" Scott asked. He took Ida Plum's dustcloth and wiped the stair rails.

"I know too much now," Ida Plum said as she headed downstairs. "Just minding my own business."

"Have it your way," he said. "But you might miss a show." He dusted so hard I was afraid he'd strip paint.

"It's only dust," I said. "Leave a little of the varnish."

"Sorry." He eased up. "My mind wasn't in this gear, or any gear for that matter. Nowhere near here." He seemed distracted. Was it something Ida Plum had said or done? Her story of Elsie Shimpock or something else? He dropped the cloth onto the cleaning cart and went downstairs. Later I thought I heard him on the phone. He was fine at lunch, calling Ida his apple pie, making sandwiches, but he didn't mention the funeral again.

That afternoon at the church the first person I saw was Elsie Shimpock, black hat and all, sitting in the last pew. I was the only other mourner and neither of us had a real reason for being here. I sat in the center section. Pastor Pittman and Father Roderick made four, and just before the service started Verna Crowell slipped in, walked by the closed casket and took a seat beside me. She wore a voile dress with a torn lace collar and gave off a strong whiff of mothballs and cedar. And Sherry. Sherry? She reeked of sweet sherry. Had she been tippling when she baked? How much did she tipple alone in her house every night of her life anyway? And maybe it wasn't such a bad way to pass an evening. I thought I might even decide to take it up . . . if I ever found time.

"I wish I could have seen Lavinia," she whispered. "It's been so many years and I wonder if she had as many wrinkles as the rest of us. I guess the undertaker took care of that, though. Now I'll never know." She took out a handkerchief with a rust stain shaped like rabbit on it and blew her nose, then folded and tucked the handkerchief in the chest of her dress.

There was only the casket spray of flowers, pink and white. I remembered Mama Alice's funeral. Though we'd requested memorials be sent to the church education fund, there had been more arrangements than I had ever seen. There was something lonely about a single spray, and the organ music didn't lift the mood. Funeral music always sounded funereal, like the organ's most sorrowful notes were pulled out and held for an even more mournful effect.

Linda Eller sat alone in the choir loft. She worked at Belk's cosmetic counter, sang for every funeral. I remembered her from high school, short, curly haired, dated Ron Eller, married the week after graduation, had a baby nine months later. Everybody counted on their fingers. It gave the town gossips exercise, kept their math working. That and bridge and Juanita's Beauty Shop. I wondered what the talk had been this week at Juanita's about Miss Lavinia's death at the Dixie Dew. Folly? Beth McKenzie's Waterloo? Who's ever going to go to a place, sleep in the same bed where somebody died? Somebody was sure to say, "That's one business that's dead before it even got started good."

Pastor Pittman took the pulpit with Father Roderick beside him and both conducted the service. They read the prescribed scriptures about everything in its time and I wondered somehow if this really had been Miss Lavinia's time. If so, would she have left such a strange note? Two words. "That is . . ." Those two words had haunted me ever since. What should I do about that note? Did it mean anything? I had been tempted to show it to Bruce Bechner, then changed my mind. He didn't seem all that quick on anything. Struck me as the good ole easygoing kind to just do what they're told, get their paychecks every Friday and keep their mouths shut.

Pastor Pittman? I could have shown the note to him, but somehow if it didn't have some president's picture on it I didn't think he'd be interested.

Now in his church he presided with Father Roderick as backup. Both men alternated with a few short prayers, and Linda sang all the verses of "Ave Maria," which really was lovely, if a little long; then they followed the casket out. As I started to leave the church I saw Father Roderick in the vestibule talking to an intense woman in a red tee-top (no bra) and tight jeans. The woman reached up, brushed lint off Father Roderick's shoulder in a possessive, familiar gesture and continued talking, her long silver earrings swinging back and forth in a fast, angry rhythm. She pulled back her long, grayish hair with a brisk toss. I noticed her clear plastic spike-heeled shoes. She was not your ordinary, run-of-the-day citizen of Littleboro. Not in those shoes.

All kinds, I thought as I walked to the door, priests and ministers work with all kinds and at all times.

"Lovely, just lovely," Verna said. She held her flat black book of a purse over her head. "It's too hot to walk to that cemetery, and if I know Lavinia, and it was my funeral, she wouldn't walk there either." She turned toward home.

I don't know why, but I decided to go on to the cemetery. To see the thing through, I guess. The rain had stopped and when I left the church I reached for my sunglasses. Everything had a bright, bright shimmer:

trees, streets, the sidewalk. I laid my umbrella on the porch swing at the Dixie Dew, heard strains of the music from *Aida* blasting from the sunporch and continued walking toward the cemetery. *Aida* meant Scott was painting the rest of the windows, which meant the Pink Pineapple Tea and Thee would soon be a reality.

In the Littleboro Cemetery, the hearse was already backed up to the mausoleum. Pastor Pittman stood beside it, Bible in hand. Off in the corner of the cemetery under a dripping dogwood tree, Elsie Shimpock watched. Like a buzzard, I thought. Lord, she's got to have some sort of empty life if going to funerals is her hobby, her kick. That woman dresses in black and creeps to funerals like a buzzard. Harmless, no one had ever known her to be otherwise, she just had a fetish for funerals. Still, she made me uncomfortable.

As Pastor Pittman finished his few verses, two men walked up: one tall and bald with the build of a football guard, sweating in a tight tan sport coat, the other wearing green polyester pants and a plaid coat in a matching green and black. He had a beaky parrot nose and small, dark eyes. They shook hands with the preacher and I heard something about "lawyer . . ." cousin . . . got

69

lost, "too late for the funeral, and where in this godforsaken place could you go to get a drink?"

I felt myself tickle out a half smile. At least they'd asked the right minister. Ask the one at the First Methodist or First Baptist and they would have gotten a frosty stare. Pittman and his parish knew their liquors and wines, where to find them. He'd probably invite these two odd fellows home, saying, "A little toddy after a rain will help get the dampness out of one's system." He'd intone, *hurmph, hurmph,* and lean the decanter their way, pouring a generous share.

There was a note on the refrigerator when I got home. Ida Plum had gone to Juanita's Beauty Shop. That's where you got the news, found out what was going on in town. The *Littleboro Messenger* came out every Wednesday, had only the old news . . . things everybody already knew, just had it confirmed. Everybody felt better to see it spelled out there in black and white. That made it official. Speeding tickets, DUIs, pocketbook thefts, bad checks, grass fires, deaths and weddings.

Miss Lavinia had gotten one paragraph on page 2, no photo, stating where she was born, that she was the daughter of so and so and the date of her death. The last line

70

read: "After leaving Littleboro, she lived abroad most of her life." Interesting, I thought, relieved that the paper had not given her the royal send-off I had imagined.

"Give me credit," Ida Plum said when she came in. "I can smell them."

"Who?" I poured glasses of iced tea.

"Father Roderick, money . . . all that. Miss Lavinia left everything she had to his church."

"So that's why Father Roderick helped with her service," I said. "And Pastor Pittman looked so pissed."

"It was considerable," Ida Plum said. "Even if you halve the figures they were throwing around in the beauty shop."

"Millions?" I asked.

"Some got it; some don't," Ida Plum said. "And even those who got it can't take it with them."

I still had to refund to the estate Miss Lavinia's two unused days from the check she had mailed to the Dixie Dew those weeks ago. Miss Lavinia's personal effects were still upstairs. Those would have to wait for the police to finish. But I wasn't going to wait or let someone have to ask for the money.

It was nearly dark when I wrote the check, put it in an envelope and walked to St. Ann of the Oaks. The huge old oak trees along Main Street cast black shadows that made me think of Halloween and spooks and here it was only nearing the end of April. I still didn't feel relaxed as I walked. Water oaks were the last trees to get their leaves every spring, remaining bare long after other trees were in full green. The oaks were also the last to let go their thin little finger-sized leaves in the fall.

I crossed the street and walked toward the parish house beside the church. Floodlights on the steeple and church roof illuminated a life-size statue of Mary in the courtyard. I was glad to see lights in the study of the parish house. I rang the bell and waited. When no one answered, I rang again. If Father Roderick had stepped to the kitchen, he might not hear the bell. Or if he had gone to his study in the church, he couldn't hear it either. I thought I saw a curtain move slightly inside the house and peeked in a window. There I saw a lamp burning near an easy chair and on a tray in front of it two empty glasses, crumpled napkins and the remains of a meal. But the room was empty.

I waited, rang the bell again, then tried the door, which was unlocked. As I went inside I called, "Father Roderick?"

I thought I heard a noise in the chapel or

in the passageway that joined the parish house to the church. Footsteps? I waited, listening to hear if the footsteps came closer. Instead they seemed to get fainter. Then silence. I heard a door open, click close.

I called again and walked through the passageway, dim with only a wall sconce or two to take away some of the darkness. The only footsteps I heard were my own. In the quiet and dark I saw a small light through the door near the altar of the church.

"Father Roderick?" I went through the door to the chapel. There I saw Father Roderick at the altar. He seemed tilted at an odd angle, half-kneeling, half-falling, half sprawled on the floor.

I hurried to him, bent and met the most anguished eyes. Eyes that didn't move but stared back at me and beyond into a world no one knew, a world as far away from the living as one could get. I called his name again, shook him. He didn't answer.

"Father Roderick?" I said softly, and shook his shoulder, more gently this time, the fabric of his robe rough and rasping against my fingers. His shoulder was still warm and very firm. I pulled him toward me and saw the flesh-colored silk and lace pulled tight around his throat. A strange sort of scarf. "What is . . . ?" I started, then stopped and quickly stepped back. The silk and lace garment seemed to be twisted very tight. I reached down to loosen it and realized it wasn't a scarf at all but a teddy. Someone had strangled Father Roderick with silk underwear as he prayed! "My God," I said. Then, "Oh God," and finally I screamed, still holding the lace straps of the teddy in my hand.

CHAPTER FIVE

Ossie DelGardo had slick black hair and was pudgy all over. Even his eyeballs were pudgy. He wasn't from Littleboro. Baltimore maybe? Massachusetts? New Jersey? I couldn't quite place his accent. He wore a ruby ring on his right little finger and tapped the glass on his desk the whole time he talked to me, his small, black eyes going back and forth over the room. He never looked me straight in the eye. The room smelled of smoke and pine-oil disinfectant. Light bounced off the pale green walls of framed diplomas, certificates and a photo of J. Edgar Hoover. All of it made my head ache.

"You're the only thing these two have in common," Ossie said. "You were on the scene. You don't look like the type, but who does? Anybody who would poison little old ladies and strangle a priest while he was praying is not your average, run-of-the-mill, day-to-day murderess."

"Poison?" I gulped. "Who?"

"The old bird. Miss Whatshername."

"Miss Lavinia?"

"That's her. We didn't find out until this afternoon. Didn't see any sense calling you in until we found out. Turned out didn't have to. You called us." He gave a sharp knife of a laugh.

"What kind of poison?" I asked.

"We don't know yet, but she died in your house, which makes me think something's going on."

"What?" I still couldn't understand. Miss Lavinia had come to my B and B and gone straight to bed. She hadn't even had a cup of cocoa unless she had gotten up during the night and made it herself, and I had not found any evidence of that sort. Maybe it was an accident. Some medication and she simply took too much, a prescription she overdosed. People that age forgot what they swallowed when they swallowed it. And she had seemed tired, distracted . . . upset about something, maybe a myriad of things. If she had been poisoned, it surely was not by me.

"Ought to lock you up," DelGardo said. "Just to keep the rest of us safe." He played with a ballpoint pen on his desk. "I been chief of police here three years and the most

I ever have to deal with is a knifing over in Queenstown one Saturday night a month, a suicide now and then, couple of teens take too much stuff . . . then you show up and I get two murders in one week. Makes work." He stood and walked around his desk, the creases sharp in his shirt and pants, his shoes polished as apples. I thought of the cowboy boots Scott wore. They'd never been near a tin of polish but were scuffed brown and tan. They looked soft with honest work.

"Makes me think I ought to go to a big city where I'd get paid enough to do this kind of thing." Ossie DelGardo turned his back to me, walked to the window and appeared to watch something outside. What could he see in the dark? Then he sat at his desk again, still with his attention on the window. What was out there?

I had been the one to call the ambulance when I found Father Roderick; then I called Ida Plum, who called Scott. Scott was there before the police came, helped me get un-hysterical and finally stop shaking.

Until Ossie DelGardo started in. Scott worked with a girl at the desk filling out papers while Ossie DelGardo took me into his office and offered me a cup of coffee . . . or something stronger, if I needed it. I did, but I'd never let him know, so I took the coffee, thick and black and bitter. I sat holding it after one sip. Then he did give me something stronger . . . a thorough grilling.

"I didn't know her," I said. "Miss Lavinia. I'd never seen her before. I had no reason."

"You wouldn't be the first innkeeper to help yourself," he said. "There's a rich heritage in the trade of robbing weary pilgrims while they sleep. Except in this case you took it all. Not a few trinkets, but the whole life."

I wanted to hit him, slap his face hard, leave it stinging, like his insinuations.

He mumbled something threatening and said, "More about that later."

I didn't like his tone. I didn't like him and somewhere I remembered something about Miranda and rights, but this wasn't official, was it? He'd offered me a cup of coffee. I was glad Ethan Drummond was on his way, though I'd hated to call him to come to the police station at ten o'clock at night. He was more used to it than me, I reasoned. After all, this was my first time. Ethan Drummond had been in law all his life. The last time I'd been in his office, we were settling Margaret Alice's estate and he'd advised me to sell the house, get what I could out of it "in its condition." He'd looked over his glasses when he said that. "And forget the bed-and-breakfast idea. It's not in the first three rules of real estate. Location, location, location. Littleboro isn't the place for it."

"I think it can be," I'd argued. "We're not that far off the Interstate, and with some advertising, listing in bed-and-breakfast directories, people will find us and come back, tell people. The B-and-B experience is unique. Think of England. It's a cottage industry there."

"The situation is different," Ethan said. "There's not competition of chain hotels and motels."

"Which we don't have in Littleboro."

"Because we don't need them in Littleboro. If a need for them existed here, somebody would have built one years ago."

"But that doesn't mean a B and B can't make it . . . once I get known in the trade." Now I knew why most lawyers and businessmen did well financially. They weren't in the least romantics. Their hearts didn't move a muscle in their heads. In fact, they probably went out of their way not to communicate with each other.

"Miss Lavinia came to Littleboro to visit friends," I told Ossie DelGardo. It's a coincidence she died in my B and B.

79

"Poison is no coincidence." Ossie Del-Gardo went to the window, pulled the blind, then turned to look at me. "Was Father Roderick a coincidence, too? There was no one in the chapel but you."

"I called you," I said. "Would I have done that if I had killed him?" I wished Ethan would get here. He probably had to dress. At least put on his shoes this time of night, find his car keys.

"Women's weapons," Ossie mused. "Poison. And silk underwear. Teddy, my wife calls it. Fanciest one I've ever seen, French label and all that . . . makes me wonder." He turned to look at me. Stared as though he wanted to see right through my clothes. His stare . . . him . . . it all made my skin crawl!

"I'm wearing my own underwear, not a teddy. Thank you very much," I said as huffily as I could. I fully expected him to ask my size, come over to me as if he'd like to check for himself. I glanced at the door, wondered if I could beat him to it if he even *tried* to touch me.

Ossie tapped his glass desktop with his ring again. "When I find the owner of all that silk and lace, I'll have my murderer, Miss Beth . . . and it might be you." He smiled a quirky little fat-cat Cheshire grin.

At that I sprang from the chair and slammed out his door. I couldn't wait any longer for Ethan Drummond's shoes and car keys. As it was, Ethan came rumbling up just as I opened the door to Scott's truck.

"There was nothing he could hold you on," Ethan said, stuffing his pajama top in his pants. "You go on now. I'll take care of Mr. Ossie myself."

Though it was only three blocks to the B and B, too much had gone on in Littleboro this week for anyone to go walking in the dark. Scott didn't say a word driving home; he just drove while I sat there and steamed like a summer storm.

When I got home, I headed straight upstairs. "I want a bath. I want to wash this day and some of the looks I've gotten from some people . . . wash them off and send them down the drain." Then I filled Mama Alice's old footed cast-iron tub with the hottest water I could stand, poured in some lemon bath salts and climbed in. I soaked and steamed and steamed some more. I was so mad. The nerve of Ossie DelGardo thinking I had anything to do with either death. He made me feel dirty with all his accusations, his insinuations, sly looks and mumblings under his breath. The way he kept playing with his desk drawer as if I laid the right amount of cash in it he'd look down, close the drawer and dismiss me with a wave of his hand. He'd close the case and not even look up as I went out. Why did I have that feeling? Because he was not "native Littleboro"? An "outsider?" Acted "big-city crime stoppers, gangbusters, TV cop, tough stuff?" He just seemed oily, that's all. Oily and slick, as if he could slide through anything he wanted or shove anything he didn't want under the table and look away.

I had loved the way Scott's truck smelled of leather and soap and oil. The kind of oil Mama Alice used on her sewing machine, a light golden and pleasant fragrance that made me nostalgic. Made me want more than ever the Littleboro of my childhood, where you could walk anywhere any time of day or night and be perfectly safe doing so. The kind of town where no one ever locked their doors, just hooked the latches on the screen doors at night and slept unafraid. There was nothing to fear. Crime and robbery were things that happened in big cities. And murder? Murder only happened in books and on the movie screens. Or television. It wasn't a real thing. Not until this week and Miss Lavinia, though it still felt unreal.

I was out of the tub, wrapping a thick,

white terry robe around me, when Scott tapped on the bathroom door. "I've made hot toddies. You'll need something. Oh, and Mr. Lucas checked in. He was late."

"Ohmygosh. I forgot him. Thank God he was late." I scooted into furry red slippers that were scuffed from all those New England winters but warm as old friends.

Scott had made cinnamon toast. I smelled it before I got to the kitchen, where he had laid place mats and napkins and wrapped the toast in a blue-checked tea towel.

"Preserves?" he asked. "I checked in the fridge, a couple of places I thought you might be holding some, and no luck."

I stepped into the pantry and came out with a jar of fig preserves. "Ta-da! How's this? Mama Alice made these last year." As I said it my throat filled up and tightened. Last summer my grandmother had bustled about this house doing a dozen things like making fig preserves and catering a wedding reception for two hundred, making the cake, ice rings for the punch bowl, cheese straws and homemade mints. Last year Mama Alice was not only alive; she was also operating at full capacity, amazing for someone heading hard toward eighty. But age was something Mama Alice didn't think about. She didn't have time. Until time stopped.

My hands shook opening the preserves and Scott took the jar, twisted it slightly, then handed it back. I took a tablespoonful and spread preserves with my knife. I tasted my childhood and summer and this kitchen and it was so good I wanted to cry.

Scott spread preserves on his toast, took a bite and beamed a satisfied smile. "God, these are good. Your grandmother knew food."

"Yes," I said. "She believed in food. Not just party foods, but fresh vegetables. Balanced meals. When I was little I thought she had scales and balanced things in each hand, I heard the phrase so much. Catering was her business and her joy. Maybe that's why she was so good."

I drank my toddy, which surprised me by being absolutely delicious. I tasted honey, lemon, whiskey, nutmeg and cream. Maybe I did need it. Though it was April and the weather was warm, I'd had a shock and a hell of a day. The toddy warmed me inside, then all over. I even felt my toes tingle, they felt so warm.

"Ida Plum told you about Miss Lavinia," I said between sips of the golden brew.

"She didn't take the time." Scott pushed the last piece of toast toward me. "But I already knew."

"When?" I asked.

"I saw Bruce Bechner at the service station. He told me."

"And you didn't tell me?"

"I didn't think it would help," he said. "You were upset already. And somebody who's thinking of opening a tearoom doesn't need a dead body in their house in the first place. Especially one who's been poisoned."

"Something like that."

He ate the toast I'd pushed back to his side of the table. "There's an auction in Cameron tomorrow. You need more chairs out there" — he indicated the sunporch — "and a worktable in here."

"Optimist," I said. "You're on if this toddy doesn't put me out until noon." Then I embarrassed myself by yawning a yawn big enough to swallow the room.

"You'll wake at eight feeling great." He collected the plates for the dishwasher and kissed me on the nose. I felt myself instinctively tilt back my head in case there was more to come, but he left. "Sleep tight, don't let the bedbugs bite," he said at the door. Scott checked the lock inside, shut the door and checked again from the outside. Then he tapped the glass, wiggled his fingers good-bye and was gone.

I sat feeling almost contented for a moment, wondering if that butterfly of a kiss counted as brotherly affection, a friendship buzz or an appetizer for something more. Whatever it meant, I only knew I was sleepy and so relaxed, limp as a rag doll. Ossie Del-Gardo and the rest of the world could go to hell. I was going to bed.

CHAPTER SIX

I did wake up feeling good, much better than I thought I would. There had been no nightmares, no reliving over again the moment of finding Father Roderick or hearing again in my mind Ossie DelGardo's hooded threats.

I didn't know what all Scott put in the toddy, but it was what I needed. Sherman was a nice way to wake up. He'd climbed on my bed, licked my cheek. Then Ida Plum. What would we do without her? Funny, in a small town like Littleboro, where everybody knew everybody else, I didn't know all that much about Ida Plum Duckett. Just that she'd worked for Mama Alice, cooking and serving, the last several years. Years I'd been away when I should have been in Littleboro, making up to my grandmother for all she'd done for me. Instead I'd gone my selfish way, sometimes not even coming back to Littleboro for a few weeks in the summer. Ben had been my life. And then one day he wasn't.

Funny, though, Ida Plum seemed to know something about everybody and more than a lot about some people. She wasn't a gossip, or didn't seem to be, worked hard and was more than dependable. She read situations, like this morning, and stayed two jumps ahead of them.

"If you're going to that auction," Ida Plum said, "eat a big breakfast first."

"Sounds like you're mothering me," I teased, and refilled my own coffee cup.

"Somebody's got to. You go running around in the dark, finding dead people and getting hauled into the police station in the middle of the night."

So I ate and dressed and was brushing my teeth when I heard Scott's truck, and his two-note whistle, at the back door.

"Ida Plum Dumpling." He circled her waist as she stood at the stove. "How come you never got married again?"

"Well, it wasn't because I wasn't asked," she said. "Maybe they never said it in the right way. And with the right jewelry." She laughed.

Scott poured himself juice. "Oh, I see. Mr. Right has to say it the right way at the right time in the right place."

"I didn't say that," Ida Plum said as I came in the kitchen. She set a place on the sunporch for Mr. Lucas. One end was straightened up and he'd have a view of the back garden. Maybe he wouldn't notice the screen I had hiding my small collection of unpainted tables and chairs. They sat stacked in an assortment of styles and finishes.

On the way to the auction Scott drove down country roads in a part of the county I didn't know or, if I did, had long ago forgotten. Dust stormed up behind him and James Galway played flute on the tape deck. Somehow I expected guitar or ballads or Willie Nelson, something in bluegrass. This was a paradox. There was a lot I didn't know about Scott, a whole book, a lifetime.

That gap of years when I had been away in that foreign land "up North." Where had he been? What had he been doing?

But the way he steered me through the crowd he seemed to know auctions and people. The auctioneer tipped his white straw hat as Scott and I walked past the crowd already seated under the trees.

We inspected chairs in a row beside the barn. There were two sets of four that matched, plus some odd ones missing rungs and seats. "I can't afford to have the seats caned," I said.

"Not to worry," Scott said. "I know the county's best caner and he's reasonable. Plus he takes MasterCard."

"You're kidding," I said, trying to check out the condition of some tables heaped high with glassware. One table had a tin top and turned legs.

I straightened up and stepped back into someone walking past. "Oops, sorry," I said. The woman in black slacks pushed past the crowd. A beefy-type fellow in a Harley-Davidson T-shirt followed close behind her, holding her elbow. He brushed past so close I felt the hair on his arms and got a whiff of yesterday's sweat. Somewhere I'd seen the woman before. But where? I hadn't been that many places lately in Littleboro.

Scott had gone to register for a bidding number and I tried not to stare at the couple, who stood away from the crowd in the shade of the barn.

Father Roderick. I remembered suddenly. That woman was with Father Roderick in the vestibule after Miss Lavinia's funeral. She was the one brushing lint off his jacket in that strange wifely intimate way.

"What?" Scott came up beside me. He poked his bidding card in his shirt pocket, left the number showing.

"That woman by the barn," I said out loud. "Don't look now, but in a minute."

"The one in black?" Scott said. "That's Father Roderick's housekeeper, Debbie. Debbie Delinger."

"Oh," I said, as if that explained something. Maybe even half of something. When I looked again, they were gone.

Scott got the bid on the chairs. Ten dollars each, but the long tin-covered table was $250.

"It wasn't worth fifty," I said. "You're nuts to pay that much."

"Those things are considered primitive pieces," Scott said. "And the only way you can get a buy is if nobody at an auction knows what it is."

"Wonder what Father Roderick's housekeeper thought she'd find at the auction?" I asked as Scott and I unloaded chairs in the backyard. The first thing we'd do was scrub and hose down years of accumulated crud off the chairs, then sand and mend and tighten legs and rungs, and finally the chairs would be ready for paint.

"Some people go to auctions just to be going," Scott said. "It's entertainment."

"That housekeeper and her sidekick didn't look like the type on the prowl for *that* type of entertainment," I said, remembering the

91

housekeeper's tight pants and top, her long ropes of limp and greasy hair, the blue bruised-looking tattoos on her companion's arms.

Scott laughed. "Who knows what goes on in this town?" he asked as he hooked up the water hose.

Ida Plum swept up the walk. "You been spied on," she said.

"Mr. Lucas?" I had a sinking feeling. "That's not fair."

"He sat in his car in front of the house a long time this morning," Ida Plum said. "And I think he took a photograph."

"I wasn't even here to do the hostess bit, bid him good-bye, ask how he slept and all those gold-star things," I moaned. "Do you think it was one of the B-and-B directories, a guidebook or what?" I had written them all for a listing, begging for a visit, a call, a notation. I didn't dream they'd come on the sly.

"I think he slept well, enjoyed your pine-apple muffins, approved of your 'Think Pink' tearoom and liked your grandmother's house in general."

"You did all the hostess things," I said, and hugged her. "Thank you."

"He even poked around the attic," Ida Plum said. "And looked in Miss Lavinia's

92

bedroom. I heard him."

"But that's not —"

"They said it was okay to clean it, so I did. The detective was through with it. Thank goodness I didn't have to explain a locked door and tell anyone the life and death story of Miss Lavinia Lovingood."

I took the broom from Ida Plum and swept cobwebs off the chairs. "What if he wasn't from anything connected with a bed-and-breakfast at all?"

"Don't think about it," Scott said. "Scrub that chair, fill that pail, kill that spider —"

"What spider?" I lifted my broom high, wished I'd been home to aim it at this Lucas guy, the nerve of him looking in my attic, taking pictures. And if he wasn't with a bed-and-breakfast directory, who was he?

Chapter Seven

One of the things I liked best about a small town was church bells on Sunday mornings. I loved the clean silver sound of them. I remembered how I felt hearing them as a child: that God was in His Heaven and all was right with the world in general and Littleboro in particular.

So, in jeans, sneakers and a sweatshirt, hands in my pockets, I walked toward the drugstore for a Raleigh *News & Observer.* On Sundays I wanted a fat newspaper that would last at least an hour. Overhead, the sky was an innocent blue with only a scant pastureful of cloud lambs and sheep. The April air was still morning wet and smelled of lilacs, dew wet and past their prime.

At St. Ann of the Oaks services went on as usual with a substitute priest for the day and Miss Tempie torturing the organ. Faint sounds of its agony wafted from behind the pale blue door.

"No rest for the weary," Malinda Jones said from the pharmacy window at the drugstore. "Some of us have to work Sundays." Since I'd been back in Littleboro I'd been too busy picking up the pieces of my current life, and trying to survive, fix up the Dixie Dew, and start a business to really catch up with old friends. And Malinda the same, full-time job plus a baby.

I tucked the thick Sunday *News & Observer* under my arm. "I know what you mean. How's Elvis?"

"Fat and sassy." Malinda poked a pencil in her black hair pulled into a round biscuit of a bun on top of her head. Malinda had been the first black (and female) student body president in high school. Not only pretty, she was also smart and the only girl from the class to get a full scholarship to med school at UNC–Chapel Hill. She ended up getting her degree in pharmacy. I wondered if she'd ever regretted not going on to med school. Had that dream gotten sidetracked into a marriage that didn't work? Just left with a child and the choice of taking on a fast-track career with some huge conglomerate of a drug company or coming back to Littleboro to live with her mama and have some help raising him? Whatever Malinda's reasons, they were none of my business.

"How old is he now?" I asked. Malinda had shown me pictures the first time I was in the drugstore.

"Twenty months," Malinda said. "And my mama is spoiling him rotten. If she didn't love to teach, she would have taken leave and kept him this winter. This way she's only got three months to undo all the good that nursery has done."

I laughed. Rosalie Jones was one of the few black teachers in the system, and a good one, too. Margaret Alice had all the respect in the world for her. "That woman deserves a better school system than we got here. She'd be principal or in administration anywhere else," Mama Alice said.

"Any chance she'll move up?" I had asked.

"This school system's too small," Margaret Alice said. "One high school. That's only a few administrative jobs and the coaches get those. They figure a man has to support a family. No matter that women do, too, this school board will never see it that way."

"Tell your mama hey for me," I told Malinda as I headed toward the register. Rosalie Jones had been my favorite teacher in sixth grade at Littleboro Elementary. She was one reason I majored in elementary education and taught elementary art myself until last year. Until my grandmother's death had brought me home and the Dixie Dew gave me reason to stay. I'd had offers to sell, but selling would be considered only when I was on my next-to-last breath. The offers had come in long legal envelopes on stationery so crisp it rattled like danger when I unfolded it. They were from some legal firm whose name took the two top rows of the letterhead and written "on behalf of a client who wishes to remain un-named at the moment." The offers were insultingly cheap and I told myself I'd be down to my last dime before I'd give away the only piece of real life I had left.

I rounded the courthouse corner and stopped for the circle traffic when I saw someone walking past the closed double doors of First Presbyterian Church. A woman in a long red dress hoofed down Main Street, swinging a black pocketbook on a chain. She swung that pocketbook as if she saw something overhead and wanted to knock it down and "stomp it flat," as the saying went. Reba, it could be nobody else. She's off again, I thought. Off to wherever her mind went when it got out of whack.

I walked behind her down the block. Crazy Reba owned the world at this moment. She had it on the chain of her pocketbook and was swinging it. For a moment I envied her careless joy, her wild, childlike, just plain efflorescence in just being alive. Reba heard all the birds and called back to them in their language, a singsong of sounds and phrases. "Thief, thief," she yelled to the blue jay.

"Thief, thief, thief!" the jay screamed back, then joined two other jays in a tree, and all of them sang, "Thief, thief, thief."

Reba stopped under the tree and flapped her arms, waved the pocketbook, and the birds shot out like blue sparks in all directions. She laughed and laughed, bent down and beat the sidewalk with the purse.

I glanced at the newspaper's headlines as I walked, half-listening to Reba's blue-jay screeches and dove coos, until I reached my own driveway and started toward the sunporch door.

Reba stopped at the front walk, stared at the house, then plopped down mightily, a heap of red melting into a blob. She took off her shoes and scratched her feet.

Oh God, I thought, she'll be there all day and anybody considering the Dixie Dew will take one look at her and drive away as fast as they can. Reba was not the advertising I needed. I backed out my yellow Volkswagen

Beetle, Lady Bug, slowed and rolled down my window. "Reba, can I give you a ride?"

Reba got up and walked to the car. She held a spike-heeled shoe in each hand: one black, one white. "You going to Vegas?" she yelled with a broad smile that showed the gap between her teeth where some were missing in front.

"I'll take you home," I said.

Reba looked as though she didn't know me from anybody, but it didn't matter. To her, a total stranger was a whole new opportunity.

"I can go there by myself," Reba said, and pointed toward her tree on the hill.

I thought Reba might be staying at the new group home; she looked clean, her hair freshly washed and combed smooth. Then I remembered Verna Crowell had warned me soon after I came back to Littleboro. "Keep your doors locked," Verna had whispered. "Reba just comes in and helps herself to your bathroom. She'll crawl in your tub, take a shower, help herself to all the soap and shampoo and hot water you got. Then she leaves a trail of wet towels out the door."

Verna went on to say that Reba had really scared her once. "I heard all this water running in my own bathroom and I wasn't in it. I knew there was no one in that house but me and I wasn't in the tub. I tell you, it's a funny feeling. Then Reba comes out, drying herself, singing up a storm."

"Take me to Vegas." Reba hit the side of my car with her shoe. "I said take me to Vegas, you car, you."

I reached for my gearshift but was afraid to start forward. Reba might step in front of the car. No telling what she'd do.

"I wanna see my name in lights." Reba looked at the sky. One eye looked too far left and toward the back of her head. I wondered what she really saw. Did she sleep or wander the streets all night? "I got my clothes all packed," Reba said. "A whole suitcase. Jesus give me a new suitcase. A new suitcase just like Selena Gomez got. I saw her on TV at the truck stop."

I had heard Reba hung around truck stops on the Interstate and hitched rides with truck drivers. She liked to ride. She'd ride anywhere. For a while she had a car, slept in it parked behind the Exxon station. Then it had been towed to the junkyard and Reba slept there until they locked her out. She hauled in too much food from the garbage cans at Kentucky Fried and attracted rats and mice.

"I'll take you to Kentucky Fried," I said, wondering if that would work, if I could get

Reba's mind going in another direction. And if I'd be able to get her out of the car afterward.

Reba crawled into the backseat, pulling her pocketbook after. "I want the big bucket," she said, "and a dozen biscuits, extra gravy and coleslaw." She gave her order to the air, then kept repeating it like a poem, "Big bucket, dozen biscuits . . .

"Jesus give me this necklace and earrings," Reba sang. "And a whole lot more."

Reba frequented yard sales, I heard, took anything anybody gave her, sold it from her old car as long as she had it. I had seen her parked at wide, shady places beside the roads, car trunk open and "stuff" spilling out. Somebody in town had probably given her junk jewelry to get rid of her. The necklace and earrings Reba wore looked old, heavy and discolored. The green stones shone like glass. Tacky. No wonder Reba thought she had something. And the Jesus bit. She could have gotten the stuff at a church yard sale, associated the church with Jesus.

Reba stayed in the car while I bought chicken: the big bucket with biscuits that Reba wanted. I handed them to her and she immediately opened the bucket and began to eat.

I put Lady Bug into gear and started toward home with the idea in my mind that Reba would take her chicken and head toward her tree to eat in the shade. Lord help me if she decided my front porch looked like a better place. But as we passed the cemetery Reba yelled, "Stop." And I was only too glad to do so.

"I want out here." She tried to open the door before I could pull over. "I want to eat with her."

"Who?" I said. "Wait a minute." I didn't see anyone, but Reba was out with her chicken, swinging her pocketbook and heading up the gravel path to the trees on the hill in the cemetery. I didn't see another soul in the cemetery, but knowing Reba, "her" could have been a bird or a statue or a tree or a shrub. She was one with all the elements.

In my own driveway, I sat a moment. I probably shouldn't have let Reba in the car, nor bought her chicken. This Reba was one I never knew, someone wound up with an energy that could do damage, become violent. I remembered how hard Reba had hit the car. When I got out to check, sure enough, there was a rounded fist-sized dent in the front fender. Reba had strong hands and a mind that went in all kinds of directions. Who knew what she could or would do? Could she strangle Father Joe and walk over his body like a pile of wet towels? Never look back or realize what she'd done? Go on to somebody else? It scared me to think about it. I'd been too close to two murder victims lately, two more than I'd ever been close to in my life, and I didn't feel too good about it.

Chapter Eight

Monday I scraped peeling paint from the doors to the sunporch, tearoom-to-be. The paint dusted and flaked all over me. My hair and my jeans and T-shirt were covered. My scraper made harsh, rasping noises as I worked. All this to get a surface ready to receive new paint. It would be worth it. Nothing seemed as clean and new as fresh paint. I even loved the smell of fresh paint. Besides, my job was better than Scott's project for the day. I heard a rumble on the roof, waited to see if he'd come sliding off, chimney-cleaning brushes at his sides like ski poles.

He'd closed off the fireplaces in all the rooms and gone on the roof with rags, rods, twisted black bristle brooms and brushes. There was no one in town to hire to do it and the chimneys had to be cleaned before the fireplace people came to start rebuilding them. "Be careful," I said when I heard any thumps and scuttles overhead.

I scraped and thought of Father Roderick. His body was being flown back to California, but the church here was holding a memorial service tonight. I wondered who'd conduct it. Who'd play the organ? Miss Tempie? Of course, she had for years . . . forever. Aged and slow, her fingers slipped and hit wrong notes in every piece she played. I'd groaned the last time I went to St. Ann's with Mama Alice. "Why in the world don't they get someone to play the organ who knows how?"

"Miss Tempie knows how," Mama Alice said. "And the church also knows to unseat her would devastate her, so they put up with the wrong notes. Besides, they'd have to pay someone else. Miss Tempie does it free. She always has. And the bookkeeping, too. Let's hope she's better at the bookkeeping."

"Ye gods and small towns." I said, sighing, and raising both arms in the air. "I give up. The wheels of progress passed this place right by and kept on rolling."

Mama Alice laughed. She said she could see both sides. She wanted Littleboro to stay small, be a place where everybody knew their neighbors and that still had shops downtown.

I said I would like it to stay small, old-fashioned and picturesque, but I also wanted it to be able to have a bookstore that didn't just sell Bibles and Bible-school supplies, customers to keep a tearoom in operation and enough people passing by and through to support a bed-and-breakfast. I'd talked to Mama Alice about the idea of the Dixie Dew even then, only we'd be doing it together. I wouldn't have the whole deal down on my shoulders alone.

Ida Plum was off until Thursday. "You don't need me until then," she'd said Saturday. After Mr. Lucas there had been no guests. I hoped it wasn't an omen. The practical side of me said there would be slow periods in the business, any business, as well as dry periods. So Ida Plum was right. "You don't need me, but call me if somebody else turns up dead," she said with a little laugh as she left. Her words hung heavy in the air like a dark cloud.

I was dusting the sideboard in the dining room when I heard a car door slam and saw three men coming up the walk to the front door. One of them was Ossie DelGardo. Even from the porch I recognized his uniform, his bulk and the glint of his badge. The other was Miss Lavinia's lawyer, Kingswood Heyman. I remembered him from the funeral. He carried a briefcase, his fat fingers loaded with rings large enough to set seals on letters and documents, and he jingled a chain copper bracelet on each wrist. Heyman introduced the younger, sweating polyester guy as "[something mumble], cousin of Lavinia Lovingood, Lester Moore."

I showed them into the living room. Scott had surrounded the fireplace with newspapers as well as covered the opening. I didn't explain, nor offer them coffee, though there was fresh in the kitchen. I hoped Ossie DelGardo would smell it and be aware of my deliberate inhospitable act.

Ossie DelGardo chose to sit in Mama Alice's little needlepoint rosewood chair. He looked like a circus elephant balancing on one of those three-legged stools. The lawyer and Miss Lavinia's cousin took the blue velvet love seat.

"You there," Heyman said, jutting his chin at me, briefcase balanced on his knees. "You got property that belongs to this estate." He danced his fingers on the briefcase.

"I beg your pardon." I wished now I had a cup of hot coffee to spill in somebody's lap. The nerve of this stranger, walking in, accusing, demanding.

Ossie DelGardo gave Heyman a look that seemed to simmer him down a little. Meanwhile Ossie kept taking inventory with his eyes, the gilt-edged mirror over the green marble mantel, Mama Alice's Tiffany lamp. "That real?" he asked, walked over to it and thumped the glass with his thumb as if it were a watermelon.

"Yes," I said, and cringed. "Very real."

Ossie scuffled the edge of one of the throw rugs I used to hide worn spots in the carpet. The carpet had many places so thin you could see the floor through them. "Thread-bare" was the word made manifest in this case, I thought. Guests thought the throw rugs were cute, that they added color and charm.

"I've got a search warrant," Ossie said. He pulled a paper from his chest pocket. "This fellow thinks you're holding on to something that's not yours. Not that I think anything of the sort, but it never hurts to do a little looking."

He had sent Bruce Bechner over earlier in the week to move Miss Lavinia's little car. I missed it. Such an elegant little sports car, made in Italy, I'm sure, and she'd had it flown over, parked and waiting for her at the Raleigh-Durham airport. Now it graced the parking lot behind the police station. Poor, sad little car.

"I don't know what you're looking for," I

said. "I have no idea that anything that belonged to Miss Lavinia can still be in this house. Not unless it fell between the cracks."

"That's just what we thought," Ossie said. "And you wouldn't mind us looking."

Look up the chimney, I wanted to say. See if you get a faceful of dirt. I almost wished Scott would descend like a genie, covered with soot, see if they'd startle.

The lawyer settled back, at ease to wait, but Miss Lavinia's cousin paced. I watched and thought Mama Alice would say that man looked like a little banty rooster just cocking his spurs, wanting to jump somebody. He looked like the type to do more crowing and pecking than actual damage.

Ossie pulled open a drawer in the mahogany desk and fumbled through Mama Alice's papers. He pulled open another drawer, almost dumping the entire contents. He checked under the drawers, felt down the sides, back, studied the rug again, surveyed the hall and sunporch where my paint cans were stacked in the corner next to the auction chairs. In the kitchen he checked the pantry, every drawer, cabinet, stove . . . even the oven and under the burners. He opened the refrigerator, peered in the freezer, pulled out the ice trays and analyzed each cube.

"If you'd tell me what you're looking for," I said, "I could save you time and trouble." Which should be easy because it wasn't there.

Ossie opened the door to my bedroom, summed up the stacks of lumber, cans of paint, tools, glanced at my drawing board, then shut the door and started upstairs.

I listened to him open and shut closets, drawers, go up the attic stairs and stay awhile before coming down. In my mind I could see Scott crashing through the roof, landing smack on Ossie DelGardo, and the two of them coming tumbling down the stairs like wrestlers.

"This house got any old hidden stairways, passages to the cellar?" Ossie asked after he came down. "Cubbyholes? Little wall safes?"

"I grew up in this house and never found any," I said.

Scott came in the kitchen covered with soot, his face and hands blackened. He looked for all the world like a coal miner. Ossie DelGardo sniffed and took a step away from him.

"You wanta undo these fireplaces, let me take a look?" Ossie asked Scott.

"Look for what?" Scott asked. He pulled off his toboggan and fluffed his hair. "God,

110

this stuff is not only thick and black; it sticks to you. There must be a hundred years' grime and grease and grit in those babies."

"Or more," I said.

Ossie waited for us to follow him to the living room.

Scott loosened the edge of one section of newspapers in and around the chimney.

"I can't see," Ossie said, and straightened up. "You think a peephole is enough? I think you're trying to hide something and figure I'll give up looking."

Scott tore away more newspaper. Ossie stuck his head up the hole, then pulled back, his face coated with black soot, only his eyes white and angry. He sputtered, coughed, cussed under his breath. "That's damn smart," he said. "But I'm up to your games. I'll be back."

After he left, the other two trailing behind him like cats, Scott and I laughed, thinking of Ossie DelGardo's soot face. We laughed over lunch, but asked ourselves what on earth had started those guys on such a search.

"Mama Alice always said rise above the situation," I said. "And this time I did. She would be proud of me. The nerve of those slimy, oily creeps."

Scott said he'd vacuum my paint scrapings when he did the chimney soot and finish the job if I wanted to start something else. A tempting offer if there ever was one. I'm not the neatest painter in the world. I just slap it on and get the job done, while Scott can paint for hours and never spill a drop. I handed him my brush and gloves, which he promptly laid aside. "Only sissies paint wearing gloves," he said.

I went to Mama Alice's old sewing machine in the back bedroom and picked up the pink-and-green print I'd bought for ruffled valances for the sunroom windows. I'd also bought enough for ten squares of color to go over the sheets I'd use for tablecloths. Polished cotton. I'd seen this print once in the dining room of a country club in Atlanta. Then in a picture in *Southern Living.* I might have lived in the North, but my heart never left the South. The pink-and-green print looked so clean and crisp I fell in love with it. Then when I saw the same fabric at The Calico Cottage and on sale, I knew I had to have it.

When I unfolded the cloth, a piece of paper dropped onto my lap, a small square with four words printed in black ink. My hands began to shake and my knees buckled as I stood. The memory of Miss Lavinia's little note was still a fresh memory. Those two cryptic words that were the last two she ever wrote. Tears stuck in my throat like stars, each point a spear of ice. The note read: "Margaret Alice was pushed."

Pushed! The word felt like a granite boulder rolled on me. No, it couldn't be true. My grandmother had been found at the bottom of the basement steps. Her neck had been broken and she never regained consciousness. She'd lived in that never-never land for months in that nursing home.

She'd fallen down the concrete basement steps she'd cautioned the rest of the family about all my life. She had said, several hundred times at least, "Somebody's going to fall down those basement steps and break their neck." But she was the one who fell. She was in excellent health, except for an arthritic knee. Still, there had never been the least question in my mind that Mama Alice fell . . . not until now.

CHAPTER NINE

"Who would do something like that?" I asked. I grated carrots to make carrot nut muffins.

Scott leaned against the counter, reading his mail. Lately he stopped by his post office box, then brought his mail here to read. He studied sale catalogs from Sears, Lowe's and Home Depot. His idea of Heaven seemed to be a hardware store or a lumberyard and paint outlet. "Sounds like a crank note," he said. "I wouldn't worry about it . . . just the reason behind it."

"But what if she was." I said. "I mean Mama Alice —"

"Don't think about it," Scott said. "A note like that isn't a serious threat. Just something from a sick mind."

"But how sick?"

"Well, folded in between fabric sounds more like a prank." Scott said, "I've got to wash these chimney brushes and get them back to the rental shop in Raleigh before two."

"Wash away," I said, shuffling through my mail, which included a letter from Ben Johnson, my ex something; a friendly sounding chatty note any longtime friend might have written. There wasn't a word of affection or any reference that there had ever been any. His handwriting was almost calligraphy. Slow, intense. Ben is the Luddite of Luddites, those who believe and cling to the "old ways" as the best way. No computers, no e-mail for him. He even said he thought all these electronics were polluting the airwaves. "Get the paint off your hands long enough to pick up a pen," he wrote. "You can't work all the time. You know what that does to one's mind. Not that it's ever had much of a chance with mine."

"Yeah," I wanted to answer. "Turns it to mush." And that's how I felt. I really should write Ben. We hadn't been in touch except for his Christmas Eve phone call. But all this was too much to write about. Too much to believe. This quiet, sleepy little town where a dog could leisurely and regularly cross Main Street at midday and not have a car honk at him. Well, maybe a toot or two . . . if traffic happened to be heavy.

I kept grating carrots. I'd make several

batches of muffins and freeze them. Who would write a note like that and put it in my fabric? And did it have anything to do with those two words Miss Lavinia had written before she died? "That is . . ." Strange last words, I thought. But not threatening. This note had an implied threat to it.

I had bought the curtain fabric over a month ago. The Calico Cottage was a dusty little shop with racks of patterns, rows of pins and bolts of materials that stood like huge books on the shelves. And presiding over it all was a wrenlike woman, Birdie Snowden. Could she have tucked in the note with the sales slip like she used to tuck in the cards of buttons and spools of thread when you bought cloth to make a dress, blouse or skirt? Mama Alice, who had sewed so much for me, used to say, "Sometimes I think we'd both go naked as Eve if I couldn't run us up a little something once in a while."

I ran my mind back over all the guests who had been in and out since I'd opened the Dixie Dew. There had been a dozen or so, including Miss Lavinia and that Mr. Lucas. Maybe he wasn't with a B-and-B directory after all but was some private investigator hired by someone to check me out. Stop it, I told myself. You know that's ridiculous. And thinking of ridiculous, Ossie DelGardo.

But he hadn't been in my bedroom this morning, only looked in the door. What about the two who had been with him, lawyer Heyman and Lester Moore, cousin Polyester Pants? They hadn't left the living room, I was sure. I'd stayed in the downstairs hall when Ossie went upstairs to poke around. And besides, it just seemed more a woman's thing to do, fold a note inside a piece of fabric. Somehow, I thought a man would be more likely to mail a note to you, pin it with a knife to the front seat of your car or seal it in an envelope and slide it under the door.

Could any of the cake ladies of last week have quietly slipped into my bedroom and left the note? They would have to go past me and probably Ida Plum, in the kitchen, and I was sure they didn't. I tried to think who brought cakes. Verna Crowell had been the first one. Verna had been Mama Alice's best friend, closest neighbor for sixty years or longer. There wasn't anything Verna wouldn't do for Mama Alice, or anyone else for that matter. Verna was a kind soul, not a sick mind, even if she did insist on her daily ration of sherry.

I looked again at the black ink, the letters printed in long slash-like strokes. Strange. And stranger still, it looked like handwriting

I'd seen before. Not the same handwriting as Miss Lavinia's note. Her two haunting words, "That is . . . ," which didn't make sense. This note, in a totally different handwriting, did make sense in a way. At least it was a complete sentence, "Margaret Alice was pushed." But who made their letters like that? Skinny, almost as if they had been painted with a brush.

Ida Plum stopped by to say she was going to visit her sister in Weaverville for a day or two.

"I didn't know you had a sister," I said. "You've never mentioned her."

"You just weren't listening. Of course I've mentioned my sister, Ida Clair. Many times, many times." Ida Plum wore deep blue slacks and a lavender pullover. She had a purple bow in her hair. As she left the porch, I caught sight of her purple sling-back pumps.

Since when did one wear bows to visit a sister? If such a sister really existed. And sling-back pumps? Must be a classy sister, I thought. Those sure looked like three-hundred-dollar shoes to me.

As I took the third batch of muffins from the oven, there was a tap on the back-door glass. I opened it to Malinda, who said, "I trust my nose and follow it." She helped herself to one of the warm muffins, breaking it open as she winked at me. "What's new in the trade?"

"Nobody. Nothing. Nada. Zilch. Zip. Zero. But I ain't complaining and see, I'm still swimming in hope. Fix up the old home place and guests will come."

"If you say so," Malinda said. She wrapped another muffin in a paper napkin and put it in the pocket of her smock. "This baby is my three o'clock snack and Lord-help-me-make-it-to-five." She slipped out the back door. "See you around."

A dozen times it had been on the tip of my tongue to tell her about the note. And something stopped me. I didn't know what. Maybe I thought it sounded so juvenile. So Nancy Drew. And yet every time I thought of it, I got goose bumps. Nobody in this world had a grudge against my grandmother. Nobody.

It was after four when Scott got back. He'd rented a wallpaper steamer to use on the hall walls. I worried we'd have to peel and scrape for days.

I had no guests, nor inquiries from any, but then it was only Monday. Things would probably pick up toward the weekend.

When he asked about Ida Plum and I told him she was visiting her sister, Ida Clair, he stopped unwinding the steamer cord and laughed so hard he bent double.

"What?" I asked. "What's so funny?"

"Don't you remember that old Knock Knock joke about who's there and the answer is 'Ida Clair'? 'Ida Clair who?' 'Ida Clair I'm from the South; who are you?"

"Okay," I said, "but that still doesn't tell me anything. And she was dressed up. A bow in her hair and heels!"

He laughed some more, slapped his side. "She really did it. She's taking the tour."

"Tour?"

"Yadkin Valley vineyard tour. It's a day thing. I gave her the flyer. Just didn't think she'd take me up on it. The wine tasting and all. Good for her. Maybe she'll meet somebody. One can get lonely, you know."

Before I could answer he started the steamer. Somehow I never thought of Ida Plum as lonely. Scott, either. Maybe I had gone around too long thinking I owned the rights to the condition.

Scott and I worked with the steamer until after midnight. There were six layers of wallpaper that ranged from bamboo to roses, the bamboo being the oldest and hardest to remove. "Remind me never to plant any of this stuff," Scott said. "I've seen enough to last a lifetime."

120

"Think how the kudzu would give it a run for the space," I said. "You know the old story about if you plant kudzu in the rear of your yard it will beat you back to the house."

Scott laughed as he left.

A few minutes later I let Sherman in the front door. I started to lock the door when I saw a huge van careen around the corner and down the street. A do-it-yourself rental type of moving van, going much too fast, and where on earth did moving vans go at this time of night? I watched as it passed and gunned down the street. I thought the determined driver looked a little like Father Roderick's housekeeper.

But what was Father Roderick's housekeeper doing driving a moving van? Ida Plum had said she'd been someone he took in and gave a job to. She probably didn't own more than the clothes on her back. Odd. But I could have sworn that was his housekeeper driving hell-bent for somewhere behind the wheel of that truck. It was her or someone who looked enough like her to be her twin sister. Two of those women in this world would be tough to take, I thought, and I didn't know why I thought that. Just a feeling. I really didn't know why the woman bothered me. But something about her bothered me a lot.

CHAPTER TEN

I hated lawyers' offices, even Ethan Drummond's old wood-paneled, pine-smelling, green rubber-tiled reception room. It looked like it had the first day he'd opened the practice with a green plastic sofa, two boxy brown plastic chairs, plastic plants and magazines no one but a lawyer would read, except a three-year-old issue of *Country Music,* which Scott started thumbing through.

The door to the inner office was closed, but behind its milky pebbled-glass pane I saw shadows, heard voices. Heyman bellowed something about this "Hicksville of a town" and "chicken shed police department." Scott lifted one eyebrow, grinned at me. "What are we doing here?"

Someone peered from the hall into the reception room, then eased himself into a chair closest to the door. Mr. Mumble Mumble Polyester, I remembered, Miss Lavinia's cousin. He perched on the edge of the chair as if he wanted a head start should an occasion call for him to jump and run. He acknowledged me and Scott with a quick bob of his head, looked behind him as though someone might be following, then waited, holding his tan pancake of a hat over one knee of those god-awful green plaid polyester pants.

I listened as Ethan Drummond's easy tones seemed to calm Kingswood Heyman down. Ethan was used to charming juries, judges, the city council, hostile witnesses, church elders . . . anybody who sat before him. He and his wife, Miss Grace, had been friends with Mama Alice for as long as I could remember. They'd treated me like a daughter, always remembered my birthdays, Christmases . . . every occasion. They thought me and Ethan Clay, their son, would marry. We would go up to the university together after high school. He'd finish law school, pass the bar, we'd get married, come back to Littleboro to live, and Clay would take over his father's practice. But it hadn't worked that way. Clay had gone to England on a Rhodes Scholarship and when he came back, he'd settled in New York. Verna Crowell told Mama Alice once that Miss Grace said, "That boy's up there just making pots and pots of money and it scares his daddy to death. He thinks you can't make all that much money unless you're doing something dishonest. He thinks Clay won't come back to Littleboro even for our funerals."

I had gotten a degree in art education and signed up to teach at a school in St. Tomsbury, Maine, where I met and moved in with Ben Johnson, a green-eyed bookshop clerk who read his wares, worried about energy conservation, world hunger, nuclear waste, and wanted to live in the jungles of Brazil because they were supposed to resemble the early days of the Earth. The bookshop lost more money every month and he kept denying it, emotionally and physically. If we talked, we fought, so Ben Johnson was reading something his every waking minute. I got tired of shouldering the whole load for someone who didn't know that responsibility begins at your own kitchen table. When Verna Crowell called me to say that Mama Alice had fallen, was in the Raleigh hospital unconscious and would probably have to go to a nursing home, I came home to visit and stayed. I slept in my old bed, woke to the walls of my childhood and wanted them back. The week my grandmother died, I wrote for Ben Johnson to ship my things. They came two weeks later and I was surprised at how neatly fifteen years of my life fit into a dozen medium-sized boxes.

Ethan Drummond hadn't charged me a cent for settling Mama Alice's estate. After the nursing home bills were paid, there was little left. After the fall, Mama Alice had required around-the-clock skilled nursing care, and it didn't come cheap. I wanted her to have the best. She deserved it, and if it meant there was nothing left but the house and its contents then I would find a way to work things out.

There had never been a question in my mind that Mama Alice fell. Until that second little note landed in my life. There was no question now, just a nagging "what if?" Sometimes the words seemed to stand just behind my shoulder and whisper loudly in my ear. I tried to brush them away.

Ethan opened the door. "You-all can come on in now. I'm short a secretary this morning, so you'll have to excuse things."

The lawyer Kingswood Heyman sat huffed up and hulking in a leather wing chair. He smiled slightly at Miss Lavinia's cousin and gave a half wave with one hand, as if he'd really like to dismiss all of us.

Scott stood. I took an old wooden chair that faced Ethan's cluttered desk. I'd never seen it when it wasn't at least a hundred papers deep in stacks and folders that slid and leaned, stuck out sideways in all sizes and colors.

"Seems Mr. Heyman and his client are a little worried about some . . . er . . . missing property of Miss Lavinia Lovingood." Ethan didn't look at us; instead he fumbled with papers.

At last, I thought, maybe we can find out what all the fuss has been about. That would be a relief. I'd been accused of murder in an offhanded way, searched in an unconventional way. And I didn't know a darn thing about either or anything that was going on.

"Exactly what?" Scott asked. "What are they looking for?"

"Miss Lavinia" — Kingswood Heymen stood, loomed rather, in front of us — "traveled this time with some of her jewelry. I won't be specific, except to say it can't be found. Not with her luggage, nor her handbag, and it's not in her car. Stands to reason it was stolen, and you wouldn't be the first innkeeper to let a sleeping person be relieved of some of their valuables, and, in Miss Lavinia's case . . . her life."

Scott sprang at Heyman then and grabbed his lapels to pull him face-to-face.

"Stop," I said. "Stop."

Ethan pulled Scott away. "Son, there's no need for that. He's got no proof."

"Except the missing pearls," the cousin piped up.

"Pearls?" I asked.

"Among other things," Heyman said. "Family pieces acquired over a lifetime. They won't be hard to trace." He eyed me with a hard, unmoving stare and brushed his lapels and his shoulders, brushed away any traces he'd ever been touched. Finally, he shook himself like an unfriendly horse that had been petted.

"I've known this young lady all her life," Ethan said, "and her family before her. They're as fine as they come. You could trust her with your life. Most certainly a handful of jewelry. She'd never touch it."

Heyman pushed the cousin toward the door. The poor man looked as if he were being pulled by an invisible rope, eyes bulging, heels dragging. "We'll get this straightened out if I have to jerk all the skeletons out of all the closets in this Podunk place." Heyman banged the door so hard the glass rattled.

"Sorry," Ethan said. "That man can't get what he wants and get away fast enough to suit me."

"Ethan," I started, "you know —"

Ethan waved his hand in the air like he wanted to erase all that had gone on in this room in the last half hour. "You don't have to tell me. I know you didn't have anything to do with the old lady's death, much less some assorted pieces of junk. I got a feeling Heyman is the kind who tries to create a cyclone to try to cover up some of his own mess."

Scott shook Ethan's hand and I hugged him, smelling tobacco and the same scent of aftershave I remembered from childhood, feeling the same rough wool of his jacket against my face. "Take care," I said.

Ethan's voice followed us down the hall as he waved us out. "Bye," he said and then repeated what he'd said earlier, "You two be careful."

"I think he's right," Scott said. "People in this town have been lucky. They've trusted too long."

"Mama Alice never locked the back door in her life," I said later.

"What about Verna? Some of the other neighbors?"

"They've always been in each other's houses . . . just like their own. They'd be offended by a locked door. Think it was the snootiest, most unfriendly thing they'd ever seen." I laughed. I thought of all the times

Verna Crowell had poked her head in the back door and hollered, "Yoo-hoo, Alice," and just come on in. If no one was home, Verna had been known to borrow eggs, sugar, a cake pan, a steam iron, whatever she needed, and then return it a few hours later, laughing she bet we hadn't missed it. The whole neighborhood had had a "my house–your house" kind of arrangement. Not anymore.

Scott dropped me off at the Dixie Dew, which seemed too quiet with Ida Plum gone for the day and no guests. It was almost dusk when I realized I hadn't seen Sherman all day. I checked his favorite sleeping places, under the back steps, the sunny side of the garage, the swing glider on the front porch. Nowhere. The food I'd put in his bowl this morning hadn't been touched. That definitely wasn't like Sherman, who ate like some other cat growled behind him ready to snatch his dish away.

I checked the shrubbery around the front hedges, calling, "Kitty, kitty!" as I went. Sherman was named after the Civil War general and Southern scourge, William Tecumseh Sherman. I could scold, "William Tecumseh, stop that," and it usually worked. Right now, I just wanted to find the cat. I wondered if I yelled, "William

Tecumseh, come here right now," the cat would appear at my feet.

When I'd checked out the grounds around the Dixie Dew I started down the street toward Littleboro Cemetery. Sherman and Robert Redford had been known to romp over and around tombstones, hide under cedars and pounce at each other. Sometimes I thought Robert Redford saw himself as another cat, one with longer ears and a short tail. That rabbit was a riot. Verna Crowell sounded so funny when she talked about him. "I was sitting there watching TV, me and Robert Redford, when the news come on about that young Kennedy boy. I thought Robert Redford was going to jump right off my lap. It scared him so."

I walked inside the wrought-iron gates and up the gravel drive, calling Sherman. That cat, I fussed. If he'd decided to take a nap somewhere he'd wait for me to find him and, when I did, he'd simply yawn, stretch himself out and allow me to pick him up and carry him home.

"Sherman!" I called. God, I hoped I wouldn't run into Miss Tempie. Surely she didn't come this time of day to put flowers on her dog's grave. Creepy, I decided. Verna might love Robert Redford, she might make a fuss over him, but she'd have enough sense not to put flowers on his grave when he died. And not to expect to bury him in a "people" cemetery.

The Merritt mausoleum stood dark in the shadows of cedars and dogwoods. I thought I saw something move behind it. I called again. I stood between the Merritts' mausoleum and the Lovingoods', wondering if it was too early for copperheads to be out. Leaves had piled up and decayed next to the side of the building. God, the things were spooky. I heard a noise, went around the corner and saw the brass door of the Merritt mausoleum was open. "Sherman!" I called. "Robert Redford!" I wrapped my arms around myself and felt utterly stupid. Here I stood in a cemetery in the almost dark trying to find a cat and a rabbit. No way was I going inside that thing to look. Besides, if it was dark out here, it would be pitch-dark in there. The cat, if he was in there, could just stay. He would come out when he got good and ready.

I turned to go back the way I had come, between the cedars and mausoleums, when I heard a scratching in the leaves. "Sher—" I started. Then I felt something hard and heavy on my head. Something that hurt like hell.

Who? Why? That was what I thought when

I woke to the darkest dark, a zinger of a headache and a smell that nauseated me. A smell that was dank and cold. Basement? Was I in the basement? I felt the wall beside me. Cement. And under me, cement. I tried to stand and bumped my head hard . . . the ceiling was cement. This was no basement. I felt the wall on my left side. My God. It had to be the mausoleum. What was I doing in the dark inside a mausoleum? I remembered the door was open and I had called Sherman and heard a noise.

Door. Mausoleums had doors. I eased my way along the wall, feeling it with my fingers, not daring to feel or touch anything else. The door had slammed shut by mistake, surely, and I'd fallen. That's why my head hurt. I felt all around the door. Every crack and seam. I felt it top and bottom and in between. My heart hung tight in my chest, fluttering as frantic as a trapped bird. There had to be a catch somewhere I could trip with my hand. All I had to do was touch it and the door would open.

Calm down, I told myself. Think. Think logically. Pretend you are blind and you're feeling for the doorknob. Start at the top, go straight across, then move down. Measure with your fingers so you'll know you're covering the surface. Go slowly, slowly. You know it has a knob. It is a door. It will open. All you have to do is find the knob.

My fist found where the knob was on the outside. Inside there was a smooth plate. No one opened a mausoleum from the inside, I realized with dread. No one ever came out of these things. They were one-way. In forever. Forever.

A little ribbon of light lay in the corner and . . . eyes. The eyes moved closer. That was when I screamed.

CHAPTER ELEVEN

The eyes jumped back at my scream. Whatever it was, my scream had frightened it. An animal of some sort? Oh, that it was Sherman. If I had to die in this box, I'd at least have my arms around something familiar. That was the smallest of comforts . . . if there could be any in this situation. But if it was Sherman, he wouldn't have jumped back at my scream.

The animal crouched in the corner. I stayed very quiet, very still. Then I heard soft thuds on the floor. Thuds that had the rhythm of hopping. Rabbit hops. Robert Redford. That darn rabbit! I called and he came to me. I gathered him into my arms. He felt warm, as glad to be found as I was to find him. "You crazy rabbit," I said, hugging him. "What are you doing here?" If only Robert Redford were a dog. He could bark. Someone might hear, come and let us out. But who? Few people ever came into this cemetery during the day and certainly no one at night. The wrought-iron gates had an automatic lock and timer on them. It might be days before anyone came. By then it would be too late. I tried to think if I'd even read in the paper of any funerals scheduled here this week. I couldn't think of any. Not many people used Littleboro anymore. Except for the older families in town, and there were fewer of them every year. Most funerals were held in the new memorial park on the other side of town. It looked like a golf course except for the statue of Jesus on a pedestal that stood in the middle.

I eased my fingers along the crack of light that was the door's edge. It was a faint light now and fading fast. Soon all would be dark. I held the rabbit close. He nuzzled my cheek, nipped at my hair.

The door was solid metal. And this one would probably be sealed even tighter except it was old and the ground around it had probably settled over the years. How much air did I have? How long could I last? And how long would it be before someone found me? What if they never did? There were no more Merritts left to bury. The mausoleum might not be opened for a hundred years and only then to move it, build a superhighway or shopping mall. Not a lot of chance of Littleboro growing to that anytime soon. Who'd even care whose bones were here in the mausoleum? If only I'd called to Scott I was going to look for Sherman, that I was going to the cemetery. Scott would never think to come here. He'd report me missing, as in kidnapped. I was an adult, or at least I thought I was most of the time. I wouldn't even get my picture on the post office bulletin board, or on a milk carton. My features and my bones would fade to dust in this cement box.

I felt moisture on the walls. If I had to lick the walls to stay alive, I'd do it. I'd do anything to stay alive until somebody found me . . . if I couldn't get out.

I put the rabbit down. He hopped back to his corner, probably settled down to sleep. He didn't know where he was. I wished I didn't.

I felt under the door. Dirt. Could I dig my way out? Maybe if I dug under the base it would be enough to unsettle the rest of the concrete. Maybe the walls were so old they'd crumble. Why couldn't they have been brick instead of cement? Why couldn't the Merritts have built a cheap mausoleum? Why couldn't they have used cheap materials that would age and crumble with time?

No, this stuff was probably better built than a bomb shelter. "Sealed tight as a tomb" was no cliché. It was true.

I dug until my wrists ached, all my nails felt broken and my fingers felt raw. I couldn't tell if I had made any progress. That was when I began to bang the door. In desperation I screamed, cried, then fell exhausted in the dirt. Dirt that smelled rank and moldy, old as death.

Then I thought I heard something. I didn't know what . . . something. Or someone?

A small, tinny sound. Closer.

A faint voice.

"Help!" I screamed. "Help me! I'm locked in here."

The voice stopped. Oh God, I thought, I've scared them away. They'll think it's a ghost. I yelled the wrong thing. "It's Beth," I yelled again as I pounded the door. "Can you help me?"

Finally a small voice said, "Who? Little Beth McKenzie?"

Verna Crowell.

"Yes!" I called. "It's me and I'm locked in the Merritt mausoleum. I'm locked in. Go get help!"

"I don't know how," Verna said.

"Call the emergency number in the phone

book," I said. "Call the police; call Scott; call anybody who can get me out."

"Be calm, be calm," Verna mumbled. "I want to find Robert Redford."

"He's with me," I said. "Get help. We're both locked in here."

"Don't cry," Verna said.

I didn't know if she meant me or Robert Redford.

"Stay right there," Verna said. "It's too late to be out. People shouldn't be running around in the dark."

She sounded addled and strange.

Surely she would bring help, I thought. Verna is old and her mind gets fuzzy sometimes, but she can still function. I hoped.

I leaned against the door. What if Verna had been the one to push me in here? What if she had been the one who locked the door? No, she wouldn't do a thing like that. Not Verna. But who? There had been two murders in Littleboro in a week and almost a third. Mine. I wrapped my arms around my knees, drew myself up small and tight.

Danger was too close to me now to be called anything but real. "Danger" was a *d* word. Like "death and "divorce." And "done-in."

Later Verna would say it was such a lucky

thing she happened to be out looking for Robert Redford and found me. She'd say, "Why, Beth McKenzie and the rabbit could have died in there." Add that it was so odd how that door accidentally slammed shut and locked. It never happened before and how on earth did it ever get left open in the first place? She'd say, "Robert Redford saved Beth's life."

I didn't see it quite that way. I knew someone hit me on the head. I could touch the swollen spot, feel the scab forming where my scalp had been torn. I didn't fall. I was hit and pushed.

Verna had called the number listed for the cemetery. She got the caretaker, who rattled up in his truck and unlocked the mausoleum door, grumbling all the time that nothing like this ever had happened before and if this was a prank he'd like to find the person who pulled it. When he did he would give them the back of his hand. And then some.

Scott went to the cemetery the next morning looking for anything that might have been used to hit me. He came back with a smooth, blunt stone smeared with blood on one side. "I feel better doing my own detective work," he said. "I don't trust Ossie Del-Gardo as far as I can throw this rock."

I discussed with Scott whether to report it

to Ossie DelGardo. This had been an attempt on my life. But somehow I felt Ossie would accuse me of hitting myself, crawling in the mausoleum and pulling the door shut after. And worst of all, he might report it to *The Mess* and there it would appear in black and white for the whole county to read: Beth McKenzie Henry, owner of the newly established Dixie Dew Bed-and-Breakfast, reported that she had been attacked . . . by a rock? What? What would it be called? Assault with a deadly rock? Confinement in a mausoleum? Great publicity for a new business. Plus I could just imagine Ossie and Bruce laughing their heads off down at the police station, asking, "What's that idiot girl gone and done now?" The less I saw of Ossie the better I felt.

Had the rock been used to kill Sherman? My head felt heavy and aching. Even my arms felt weighted. I drank coffee on the sunporch, thought how yesterday my big job was to steam off the rest of the wallpaper and see how many chairs I could paint. Today it was to stay alive and try to find out who wanted me otherwise and, most of all, why?

I couldn't think why I'd be in danger. Sure, there had been two murders in Littleboro, but I'd never seen Miss Lavinia before

140

last Sunday night. As for Father Roderick, I had visited his church. I'd seen him cut across the corner sometimes when he came from the tennis courts over at the high school. That was the extent of my knowledge of Father Joe Roderick.

"There's something rotten in this town," said Scott. "Somebody has got to find out what and who's causing it. I don't think it's going to be Ossie. He didn't sign on for this."

"There's a connection," I said. "Somewhere a thread, a link . . . and it isn't me. It can't be me."

"The only link I see," said Scott, "is that Miss Lavinia left everything to Father Roderick's church."

"But what about her jewelry?" I tried to eat a slice of toast, instead buttered it once, twice, set it aside, then broke off a corner and chewed it absentmindedly.

"Mr. Polyester, the crazy cousin," said Scott. "He must get the jewelry or he and the lawyer wouldn't be hanging around."

"None of it makes sense."

"Does murder ever make sense?" Scott poured me a cup of coffee.

I hoped it would be enough to get through the day, though I felt like it would take the whole pot.

"Think it's safe for me to go to the super-market?" I asked at about four o'clock.

"If you don't go near any cemeteries," said Ida Plum, who had heard of my escape and stopped by to see the remains. "Sometimes I think you need one of those Lifelines around your neck. You get in more trouble. Where was your cell phone?"

"On the kitchen counter, of course. But I don't plan to ever go near another cem-etery," I said, taking car keys from my purse. Until I'm carried to one. But I didn't say that aloud. It was closer to the truth than I wanted to think.

CHAPTER TWELVE

"They stripped it," Verna said. She stood next to the produce counter and balanced a cabbage like a head in her hand. "Weight," she said, and lifted it as if she wanted to look it in the eye. "That's what you feel for. Solid for its size." She held the cabbage out, then palmed it like a bowling ball before putting it in her cart.

"Stripped?" I rolled a dozen apples into a bag. I didn't have my mind on shopping or on Verna. That morning I had found Sherman asleep on the backseat of my car. He had probably been there all the time, knew a good place when he found it and decided to stay. He'd only yawned when I lifted him out and hugged him.

"The housekeeper and that leather-jacket boyfriend of hers. Joe Roderick didn't have any sense about people. Took in anybody off the streets." Verna leaned close into my face, her breath smelling dry as oats, heavy as molasses. "If you ask me, and nobody has yet, but they will, that housekeeper was up to something." She broke two bananas off a clump and laid them in her cart. "Poor man. Too innocent for his own good."

Verna pointed to the remaining bananas. "Honey," she said, "I hope you cut the tips off your bananas when you get home and wash them good with soap and water. You don't know where they might have been."

I counted out three lemons and put them in a bag. "What did the housekeeper take?"

"Everything, honey, everything," Verna said. "Every dish, spoon, speck of lint. I guess they left the light coming in the windows, but that was all." She laughed. "Lord, that took gall or guts or both. They just cleaned out the rectory . . . couch, chairs, tables, beds, rugs, lamps . . . they took everything but the curtains and shades." Verna squeezed a tomato. "I guess that's one way to get your house cleaned, but I can do without it just the same."

I remembered the moving van at midnight. "What would make anyone do a thing like that?" I wondered aloud. I moved my cart to the celery and carrots tucked in their shining plastic bags and separated by nosegays of curly parsley. Mama Alice always believed parsley set off anything you served, whether it was sandwiches, soup or just eggs and toast. And she grew her own, year-round. There was a sunny spot by the kitchen door that had been her parsley bed for years. I used it for greenery with the fresh flowers I put in every guest room.

"Who knows why anyone does anything anymore?" Verna answered, pushing her cart toward the cheese and dairy.

Miss Tempie, in a green organza dress, wheeled past. Half of the handkerchief hem swept the floor behind her like a train. She wore a matching hat that had been shoved too close to the side of the hatbox during storage. The rim of it tilted up on one side and the giant pink silk poppies spilled down the other. Miss Tempie had her nose in the air as if she smelled something unpleasant and was trying to get out of its range. In her cart she had two cans of cat food, a head of lettuce and two blank cans missing their labels and bent in the middle. I thought about Scott saying half the little old ladies in Littleboro lived on cat food and socked away their savings or dropped them heavily in the various collection plates around town. Unless Miss Tempie had taken in a stray cat lately, she was one of them. Eccentric, I thought. Probably counts every penny, sits down every month and balances her checkbook to the last cent, then she never knows how much she's got in stocks, bonds, trusts, real estate . . . whatever. Who knows how much she's worth? Her family had owned half the town at one time, the Lovingoods the other half.

"Hell to pay," Miss Tempie said as she wheeled past. "Everything has to be accounted for."

I thought she looked paler than usual, her eyes as dark and angry looking as two burnt cookies.

Verna pulled herself up small and close to the side of the dairy case. She wrapped her arms about herself and tried to look blank. I thought I heard her let out a breath of relief when Miss Tempie passed without seeing her. What was Verna afraid of?

"It's not that cold in here," I said. "Even with the air-conditioning."

Verna shook, briskly rubbed her shoulders. "I just never get used to it . . . air-conditioning." She looked at the ceiling. "I must be standing under a duct." She glanced behind me. "Lord, there's Reba. Let me get to the other side of the store before she sees me or she'll end up following me home."

"Got my medicine," Reba sang as she swept past. "Best medicine in the world."

She held a bottle of grape juice tight to her chest. Reba wore jeans, a black T-shirt that said: "We're the Monkees" on it and some sort of cape that had once been part of an orange blanket, a wild orange, as if it had been dyed with full-strength tangerine Kool-Aid. Reba trailed the blanket, whose back edge had raveled to a fringe. She click-clacked her rubber flip-flops like a child smacking bubble gum. "Gotta move this train along." She swung her cape around.

She's out of it, I thought. Poor Reba. One eye looked toward the ceiling. The other one studied the produce counter. Did she see anything at all? Reba shook her hair, which had leaves and twigs entwined in it, and I saw that she wore the longest, tackiest earrings ever molded and glued. They were tarnished black and had green plastic "stones" big as half dollars. Reba jiggled her feet as she stood in line. "At the junction, Petticoat, that is." She whoot, whooted like a train.

She's been watching reruns on TV, I thought. She can probably sing every theme song from every sitcom that's been on television for the last twenty years, including, apparently, *Petticoat Junction* and "Hey, hey, we're the Monkees."

Verna put a loaf of bread and English muffins into her cart and headed for the check-out. In line she picked up a tabloid. "Queen Sees Elvis in Her Private Pantry," read one headline. "Twelve-year-old Gives Birth to Three-Headed Dog," read another.

Outside, I looked for Verna to see if she needed a ride home. Miss Tempie seemed to be long gone. Reba sat on the curb in front of the store, playing with her toes and drinking grape juice from the bottle. She seemed happily absorbed.

"Eeenie, meenie, miney, moe," Reba sang. "Out you go, you little piggy, you."

She didn't see me as I got in the car, and I felt I had managed to escape something, I didn't know quite what. Driving home I noticed an annual spring sale sign in the Calico Cottage window. Herb Philpot's Exxon had red flags flapping and Clyde Edgemont of Clyde's Used Cars propped one leg against the side of a gleaming black Buick. I knew he told customers this was the finest car ever to cruise a road and no sirree, it didn't use a drop of oil. Not the first drop he knowed of.

I parked around back. Scott had screens off the windows, a ladder to the roof and the hose in his hand. He had washed the windows and screens. Scott was spring cleaning from the top down. Maybe my

Lady Bug would get a scrubbing, too. But that was something I could do myself. I always had.

I lugged the bag of groceries up the back steps to the screened porch. These weren't steep steps compared to the concrete ones in the basement. Still I felt slightly breathless when I reached the top. All my life I'd been cautioned about these steps and the basement ones. I'd never fallen . . . nor had anyone until Mama Alice. I tried to imagine Mama Alice in a heap at the bottom of the stairs and felt a chill like Verna had in the grocery store. How long had Mama Alice lain there cold and in the darkness before she'd been found?

The furnace man had found her. He'd come to check the furnace. Mama Alice never locked the back door and he'd used it all his life, like the plumber or anyone else who needed to. He had gone next door to get Verna and Verna called me in Maine. I had taken the first flight and thanked my lucky stars that my grandmother had been found not too long after her fall. Mama Alice had lived longer than she'd wanted to. I was sure of that. Something told me. She was locked in that body that took its time dying.

I spent those months holding my grandmother's hand, putting cracked ice on her lips, talking to her, reading aloud, pretending any moment she'd wake as though she'd been asleep. Maybe Mama Alice didn't know if I was in Littleboro or New England, but I knew. There were nurses to do what nurses do best, but I was there. Mama Alice was clean, comfortable, cared for. She was in no pain, only a place between living and dying, a place that was no place at all.

I shelved the rest of the groceries, put the milk, apples, butter and odds and ends in the refrigerator.

Scott yelled for me to raise a bedroom window and unlatch a screen. He stood outside on the ladder. I told him about Father Roderick's housekeeper and the whole house theft.

"Maybe she didn't get her wages," Scott said. "Decided to take it out in furniture."

"White-collar crime?"

"Black turtleneck," he said. "How'd they discover when it happened?"

"Verna said one of the church members called and couldn't get anyone on the phone, so she walked over to see what was going on. That's when they saw the place was completely empty."

"What was going on had gone, huh?" asked Scott.

When I'd seen the moving van tearing down Main Street I should have called someone. Neighborhood Watch didn't work if neighbors only watched and didn't do anything. I'd thought it an odd hour for a U-Rental truck to be hauling ass through town and that the frantic driver had looked familiar.

"Where was Miss Tempie?" Scott asked.

"She doesn't work on Mondays." Miss Tempie wasn't beyond suspicion in my book of doing anything or arranging to have it done. But maybe I was just remembering those piano lessons with the alcohol and ruler. They had left their mark on me. Permanently.

Scott carried the screen down the ladder. "This is the last one. I'll leave it with the others to dry. Gotta go pick up something at the warehouse. Be back in about an hour."

I waved, said, "See you," and headed upstairs.

In the upstairs bath I checked the tub for cleanser scum. I always felt like Mama Alice running my fingers over things, checking for little details. Sure enough, I picked up white dust. I got a cloth and polished the sink and tub. I didn't like to take a bath with cleanser scum and I didn't think guests would either. Guests. I hadn't had any this week. Had word gotten around in the trade? Was Ossie DelGardo whispering through some underground that mysterious things were happening around the Dixie Dew and attempts had been made against me? Be paranoid, will you? I looked in the mirror. I had dark smudges under each eye as if wild mushrooms had sprouted there overnight. My hair needed a trim and a shampoo. Most of all, my face needed a smile. I pushed up the corners of my mouth. Fake it, kid, I told the girl in the mirror. You're here. It's got to be a whole lot better than where you were about to spend last night, not to mention the rest of eternity.

Then I heard a light tap, tap, tapping on the window.

"Scott?" I raised the window. "Scott?" I called. I looked down. Even the ladder was long gone and the air thoroughly empty.

Was I hearing things now? Had Crazy Reba followed Scott up the ladder to look in my bedroom window? Then moved it? Whoever it was had to be bold to do it in broad daylight unless it was someone we all knew who could go about and never be suspected. You can live in a small town most of your life, know everybody and who they're married to or related to, and then something happens and you find out you really didn't know some people at all.

CHAPTER THIRTEEN

When I reached the backyard there was no one to be seen. As I rounded the corner toward the front of the house I saw something gleaming under the shrubs. Sherman pawed it. He was always chasing lizards. "Stop it," I yelled at him. "Bad, Sherman, bad." I picked up the cat, but the black-green shiny object didn't scoot away. "Run for your life, lizard," I said while Sherman squirmed mightily under my arm. I touched the lizard with my foot and still it didn't move. I sent Sherman around the corner and bent to pick it up. Not a lizard at all, but part of an old earring, blackened silver with a slender green stone. The earring felt heavy in my hand and looked very expensive, maybe even real? I tried to polish it against my shirt but couldn't tell any difference. Though it was too heavy to be plastic, the earring still looked like something Crazy Reba would hang on herself. A real bauble.

I patted Sherman, who now rolled over on his back and waited to get his stomach rubbed. "You're innocent. And I'm sorry I ever thought you weren't. Go sun yourself. Go in peace." I could swear the cat smiled. "Sweet idiot."

I held the earring up to the sun as Scott came up from his errand. "You sun gazing?"

"Look at this." I handed him the broken earring.

"Where'd it come from?" He studied the back of it.

"Sherman had it."

"Sherman?"

"He must have found it in the grass. I thought he had a lizard and took it away. Think it's real?"

"It looks really real to me," Scott said.

"Looks like Crazy Reba to me, but where would she get it?"

"Who knows? The latest yard sale? Flea market? The dump? She forages twenty-four hours a day . . . wide and deep . . . all hours of every night, days and weekends."

"I wonder what all she sees?" Scott asked. "What she knows? Maybe she knows who killed Miss Lavinia. Father Roderick? But who'd believe her if she did?"

I remembered Reba the day I'd bought her fried chicken, singing, "Jesus give me this necklace." What had all that been about? Was this earring part of it? Maybe Reba had a key to some of this stuff going on . . . if it wasn't Reba herself. But I couldn't imagine Reba poisoning Miss Lavinia. Father Roderick? I didn't know. Reba had such strong hands and her mind was so strange.

A blue sedan cruised by, turned when it passed Verna's and came back. This time it pulled in the drive and a woman in white slacks opened the car door and yelled behind her cupped hand, "You got any rooms left?"

"Yes." I motioned her in. "We've got parking in the back."

The woman hopped out, pulling on a black sweatshirt that read on the chest: "God, I'm good." "We're half-lost," she said. "And I told Leon if he went a mile further, I'd faint on him. I'm that fatigued. There's tomorrow, I said, but Leon could drive straight into it. Some men think they've got to drive the wheels off a car the first day." She flung a huge straw purse over her shoulder and pulled on pink plastic sandals. "Shirley Putterman," she said. "And I'm pleased to be here. I could kiss this ground I'm so tired of that car."

I led her toward the hall registration desk.

The woman hollered around the porch as Leon drove in the back. "Bring that little bag, too," she called. "I need . . ."

I didn't hear the last part. "Room with a private bath or shared?" I asked. "We have no other guests at the moment, so the shared bath would be private unless someone else comes."

"We'll take a chance," the woman said, and signed the registration. "Life's a chance anyway, I've always said, and I'll even shower with somebody if I have to. Naked is a state of mind. That's how God made us and I've never been ashamed of it." She looked around the room. "Honey, this is the cutest house. Can I poke around a little?"

"If you don't mind stepping around paint cans, ladders and stacks of lumber. You'll have to use your imagination. All four bedrooms upstairs have been redone; everything else is in the process."

Shirley Putterman stood in the dining room. "That corner cupboard must be two hundred years old. Honey, where on earth did you get a piece like that?"

"My grandfather," I said. "He made it. Also the bed in your room, chest . . . the nicer pieces of furniture."

"This table must hold sixteen. It's solid, I bet."

"We don't serve meals," I said. "Only breakfast . . . until ten." I suddenly thought of Miss Lavinia, who never made it down to breakfast at all.

"We had barbecue. When Leon gets barbecue hungry and there's a place within fifty miles he can spot it. He eats." Shirley met him at the front door and patted his tummy. "That's my Pooh Bear," she said. "Upstairs."

"To the left," I said. "The green room."

"I just love it," Shirley said from the stairs. "Love it."

It felt good to have guests again. The Dixie Dew was still in business. I felt like flying a victory flag to celebrate. Don't tread on us, I wanted to say. Maybe I ought to make a flag with the slogan or some motif and fly it out front. Or different ones for every day in the week.

After Scott left and the Puttermans got settled for the night, I made myself a sandwich and a cup of tea, which I took to the front porch, then sat in the swing and took deep breaths of good, clean Littleboro air. I loved the smell of boxwoods and sometimes there was a lingering waft of Verna's lilacs.

Later that night I was reading in bed long after the house had gotten totally quiet.

There was a breeze through the open windows and the sheer curtains billowed softly. A touch of dampness to the night air made it a little too cool for me. When I got up to lower the window I saw someone standing on the corner under the streetlight. Reba? Or the ever present Ossie DelGardo? The bulky shadow moved out of the light before I could tell if the figure looked male or female. But why was someone standing there at all? Were they watching the house or my bedroom? Either one didn't make me feel very comfortable. I checked the locks on the doors. I listened to crickets and tree frogs and watched a luna moth batting the streetlight. Everything seemed normal. At peace in Littleboro. Or was something just watching and waiting with me in mind?

The next morning at the drawing board in my bedroom I steadied my hand and cut a pineapple stencil with an X-ACTO knife. I was surprised my hand didn't shake. Easy, I told myself. Slow and steady and easy. I bent over Mama Alice's old breadboard where I'd tacked the pattern with the stencil over it.

The day before, Scott had painted the sunporch linoleum jade green with dried swirls of dark green over it like shadows fringing the sun through spring leaves. It turned out better than I thought it would.

I planned pink pineapple designs in the center of every eighth block. When you can't afford new, you make do. I thought of Mama Alice who ate, slept and breathed the "Use it up, wear it out, make it do, do without" philosophy. Bless her, I thought, how much she taught me, how much she left that doesn't demand time and money and attention like the Dixie Dew. I was convinced that had Mama Alice been alive today, she would have insisted on doing a bed-and-breakfast herself. And the tearoom. She'd be beating up pineapple muffins at midnight, setting places before she went to bed . . . and loving every guest, looking at pictures of their families, sending them off with recipes and cuttings from whatever plant or shrub they had admired blooming in her yard.

When I'd cut the last curve of the pineapple stencil, I laid my X-ACTO knife carefully beside my drawing board. I held my stencil to the light and said, "Darn good. In fact, damn good," for someone who spent too much of my art training teaching kiddy balloon and papier-mâché crafts. Every day I'd laughed and hugged a hundred kids, then gone home to the most morose man in the world. More than morose, he hated everything, starting with me just because I happened to be in the room.

I said softly to the ceiling, "If it takes everything in me, I will get to the bottom of what's going on in this town. I will find out who pushed Mama Alice and who's trying to kill me. I will not live with threats on my life." I'd gone through too many years of playing Little Red Riding Hood, going down the garden path with my basket of goodies not suspecting the death wolf waited in my own hometown.

I drew the outlines of each pineapple on the painted floor.

"It's Pink Panther paint to me," Scott said from the kitchen. I hadn't heard his truck in the driveway or the kitchen door open.

I laughed. "That's better than the way Ida Plum chooses to describe it."

Scott picked up the small brush and filled the pattern with pink paint. We worked silently for the most part, surrounded and filled from fingertips to toes with good talk from WUNC Radio. I worked until my back felt bent and Scott filled in the last pineapple on the last corner.

Usually Scott would only paint with his own brushes, but he didn't have one small enough for this delicate job. He insisted no one could properly clean brushes but himself, so he took our used brushes to the basement to clean while I stood in the dining room doorway and tried to see the completed room in my mind's eye. Polyurethane would go over the pineapples tomorrow. A couple of coats and they'd be sealed to take a lot of wear, plus the shine would add light and a clean look. The one solid wall would be papered in a calico print of pinks and white and green. Valances of quilted fabric that matched the cloth napkins and complemented the tablecloths would finish it off. Elegant but warm, that was the look I wanted. Most of all filled with paying customers.

Scott came in with clean brushes. He smelled of turpentine and soap as he reached for the paper-towel holder. "You clean a good brush and it'll last," he said, kneading and stroking the bristles.

"Is it possible someone wants this bed-and-breakfast to fail?" I asked. "If it goes, I go, and another piece of fine old historic property gets eaten by the bulldozers. Who would want that and why?"

Scott popped a beer, poured it, foaming and blooming a fine head, into a glass. He sipped long and loud. "Ah, babe," he said. "You got all the puzzle pieces you need. It's putting them together that's going to take some doing."

We went out to the front porch. Next door, where the new condos were being built, the carpenters had quit early and quiet settled in on the porch. Scott and I sat in the swing and stared through the magnolia trees at the gray colonial façade. "Who in Littleboro is going to buy three-hundred-thousand-dollar condos? Somebody is going to lose their shirt . . . or petticoat, or both," I said.

The sign out front said: ALCAMY COMPANY, ANOTHER FINE COMMUNITY. It told us nothing.

"Like fast-food places," I said. "It's probably a chain. But Littleboro doesn't seem to me to be the place for condos."

"Ha." Scott sat up straight. "Think opposite. Fast food needs traffic. Condos . . . retirement condos need the quiet life. That's Littleboro."

"That *was* Littleboro," I said. "But I think you're on to something. Before last week, Littleboro was a quiet, clean, green place in which to be part of a community, play bridge or go to Pinehurst to golf . . . your ideal village."

"And it will be again," Scott said, "when this bizarre business gets cleaned up."

I shook the ice in my glass. "You talk like

it's a case of acne. If so, Miss Lavinia and Father Roderick got taken with it terminally." I finished the last swallow of my tea. "There are clues and I don't think Ossie DelGardo is doing a damn thing he can't do with his feet on his desk. The most effort that man puts out each week is to collect his paycheck."

I punched a pillow I'd taken from a chair and held in my lap, scaring Sherman, who jumped from the porch roof onto the top of a column, then into a cedar that swayed as he backed his way down furiously. When he reached the ground, he streaked toward the back. "Wonder if that was Sherman on the roof I heard yesterday?"

"Before you found the earring? And thought it was Reba?"

"Reba was here . . . sometime. That earring is hers and it's real. Here she is living under a tree . . . in a tree . . . whatever . . . and wearing who knows how much of a fortune in jewels."

"Only in Littleboro." Scott laughed. "All this sounds like one of Ida Plum's stories . . . except the murders. Ida Plum's stories never had violence. They were just bizarre and crazy and strange and loony."

"Reba's a little puzzle piece we can work with," I said. "She fits somewhere. That

164

jewelry belonged to somebody."

"Jesus," Scott said. "Remember, Reba said Jesus gave her that necklace."

"Oh Lord," I said. "And Jesus saves S and H Green Stamps, too. Remember that old joke?"

"No," Scott said, and laughed. "But both of us are thinking in the back of our minds that it's a possibility Reba is trucking all over town loaded to her scalp with Miss Lavinia's jewelry. What a hoot! Who would believe it?"

"I believe it," said I. "And my good name goes riding along with her. Oh Lord, does it?"

When Scott left, I stood on the porch for a few minutes. Sherman rubbed my ankles until I picked him up.

A part of me wanted to ask Scott to stay. To say we'd make dinner, something hot and peppered, full of garlic and herbs, and then . . . I didn't know what came after that. Or what I really wanted to come after that. So I watched his blue truck zip up the street, around the courthouse and completely out of sight. I stopped my train of thought before it jumped the track and headed toward the river or someplace more dangerous in my life.

CHAPTER FOURTEEN

The next morning I stood before the drugstore jewelry counter with twenty dollars in my hand. I missed "dime stores," the Roses stores, McLellans and Woolworths I'd grown up with. Littleboro had one of each and I'd spent Saturday mornings with fifty cents to spend among the marshmallow peanuts, Blue Waltz perfume sets and rhinestone hairnets. Usually I bought books of paper dolls or wonderful, waxy-smelling boxes of crayons or magic brush paint books.

"Ah," said Malinda. "A big-time spender. Got me a live one, Mr. Gaddy!" she called to the back. Then to me she said, "I'd rather sell rings and things than peddle pills." She slid on a dozen jangle bracelets, held both arms up like a snake charmer. "This is usually Delores's counter, but she's off this week. Went to see her son in Alabama. She'll never recognize the place when she gets back. What can I sell you?"

"The cheapest, tackiest, wildest junk jewelry you got," I said.

Malinda laughed and reached behind her to a box heaped high with every color of plastic made to jangle or wear on ears or string like Christmas lights around your neck. "This box has been waiting for a sucker like you. I'd say it's waited as long as it can without scenting up the whole place." She pulled out a huge pink plastic chain and held it up. "Think this will fit? You planning on the country club dance or something?"

"Reba," I said. "They're for Reba . . . not me."

"For a moment there I thought you'd left your taste back in third grade." Malinda plowed with both arms through the jewelry. "Give me twenty dollars and this entire box of priceless jewelry is yours, and yours alone."

Malinda dumped the contents of the box into a brown bag for me. "Tell her not to wear it all at one time or she'll be arrested for tacky." She folded down the top and handed it to me. "Is it Reba's birthday?"

I hesitated. "I wish it were that simple." Should I tell Malinda? For some reason I felt if anybody in town could be trusted with the truth, it was Malinda. So I told her about the jewelry, and Malinda leaned her head back and laughed. "For a quiet gal you sure do get in some messes." Then she asked seriously in a low tone, "And what do you do with the real things after you get them from Reba? Turn yourself into a target?"

"I think I know who the real things fit," I said. "And if I can't get them back to their owner, I can at least get them to the next in legal line and get some DelGardo hassle out of my face."

"Good luck," said Malinda. "And let me know what happens?" She waved me out the store, glanced behind her and whispered, "Take care, you hear."

Now to find Reba. Should I try Reba's tree or first try to guess where Reba might be? The Dinette. Sometimes Blue's Dinette behind the courthouse fed Reba. The meal was pay to keep her away during their busy hours.

I put my face against the plate glass and shielded my reflection with one hand on my forehead. The lunch crowd was lawyers sleek in their dark suits and paisley ties, visiting judges, defendants, telephone linemen, construction workers and anybody in town who liked their food Southern fried and floating in gray grease. They ate there.

A plate of greens, the dried beans of the day, sweet potatoes, fried okra, corn, corn bread, all went for something like $5.50. Tom Blue and his son John Robert cooked six days a week in a blackened back room, passed the plates over a swinging half door and kept half the county fed. Including Reba if she ate in a back corner and kept quiet.

Sure enough, I saw Reba, Kool-Aid blanket-shawl and all, in a back corner swigging the last of her iced tea. I waited. I sat on one end of a stone bench under a budding dogwood tree in front of the courthouse and waited. Reba would be by, two or three toothpicks in her mouth and smiling like an otter. I pulled out the largest, loudest bracelet and necklace and laid them on the bench. Bait the trap, I thought. Spread honey for the strange orange bear.

Reba did look bearish and bulky in her blanket as she swaggered, full bellied, down the walk. She spotted the bracelet like a hawk drawing bead on prey. "Mine?" she said, and swooped.

"Yours," I said. "You can have it."

Reba slid the bracelet on her arm, twirled it around a little and danced, then reached for the necklace. "Mine now."

"If you want them," I said.

169

"Pretty Reba." Reba patted the necklace to her chest.

"Want me to fasten it?" I asked. "Turn around."

I lifted Reba's hair that was heavy with dirt and oil. Underneath Reba's ragged sweatshirt I felt several necklaces. "You want these old ones off?" I asked. "Aren't you tired of them? You got new ones now."

"Off," Reba said, and pulled at them.

I took off a dozen necklaces of various stones and metals. There were jeweled pins inside Reba's blanket that glittered like a swarm of insects.

"Take them all off." Reba helped me unpin the various broaches. She laid them on the bench, giggling. "I got new junk."

I laughed. Reba saw it all as junk. She hung on earrings, three more necklaces on top of the pink plastic chain, and filled her arms with bracelets from elbows to wrists. Then she stripped rings, handed them to me and put the ones I gave her on every finger, wiggling them in front of her face like a child, giggling all the while. She danced away singing, "I got new rings and things and things and rings."

Lord, I thought, she's a flower child without a garden. She's too late. Twenty years ago some commune would have taken

170

her in. I gathered up Reba's discarded jewelry and stuffed it in the brown bag. I rolled the top down and tucked it under my arm like a loaf of bread or a ham. The stuff was heavy. No wonder Reba was glad to get it off.

Now if I could only get rid of it before somebody knew I had it. I headed home at a determined pace, but not without first looking back. What if someone in a court-house window had watched the exchange between me and Reba? Somebody could quickly figure out what I was doing and why. Somebody who did not have my best interest at heart. Somebody who had in mind another trip to the cemetery for me. This time in a hearse.

I thought rightfully my "find" should go to Ossie. But he was sure to jump to conclusions and down my throat, about me making his job harder, concealing stolen property, lying to him when I had it all along, and he, big, tough lawman, would have to arrest me. Just for hindering his investigation. I didn't know what to do. Home seemed the surest place to go, but halfway there I changed my mind. What would I do with this stuff after I got there? Put it in the cookie jar? That would be worse than having Crazy Reba roaming around town dangling it across everybody's doorstep and backyard shrubbery. I opened the bag and felt around in the jewelry I'd gotten from Reba, found the matching earring to the one Sherman had been playing with. Found a string of pearls long as a rope and so beautiful they took my breath away. Good stuff. Real stuff. Somehow I thought I knew though Mama Alice, my mother, or I had never owned anything the likes of this.

On a whim I turned toward Ethan Drummond's office. The office door was closed, and I hesitated. Was I doing the right thing? I didn't know who I could trust these days. All I knew was if I began to doubt good people like Malinda, and now Ethan, I was too fearful of the world, too timid to live in it with joy.

"Ethan!" I called.

From the back office he gruffed, "In here."

I heard the metal squeak of an ancient desk chair as it swiveled and he rose to meet me, offering a hug against his rough Harris tweed chest. "Bethie, honey," he said. "You're the last person I expected to come through that door. What can I do for you?"

"Do you still have that old office safe?"

He partially closed the door. "Anybody would have to blow up the building to get it out," he said. "And it opens only for me. Why?"

"I need to put something in it." I thrust the bag toward him. "For a few days." I read his puzzled eyes. "I didn't steal it."

"I never thought such a thing. You're not the thieving kind. Never in a million years. I'm just curious why my old safe? Why not a safe-deposit box at the bank? I'm assuming that's the last of Margaret Alice's silver."

"No," I said. "It's not even mine. I'm just keeping it until the person who has a right to it can come claim it."

"Good enough." Drummond took my package, placed it atop the safe and dialed the combination. "It's here until you want it."

"Thanks." I hugged him again, feeling the fragility of his bones and age through his coat. On impulse I kissed his cheek. "Thanks for everything."

As soon as I opened the building's outer door, I heard the string band. Bluegrass, I thought, Country and Western, and half the town would be there patting their feet, sitting on the grass as they unwrapped free hot dogs, drank Coke from red and white paper cups and tied red balloons to all the babies' wrists. The new Foodland was having their Grand Opening. Good-bye, Mr.

Murphy's M.&G. Growing up, we used to call it Mr. Murphy's Mighty Good Food. Chain stores would put all the old-time small merchants out of business. Look out, Mr. Gaddy, I thought. There's a CVS headed your way. They'll be smart enough to make Malinda manager first thing and pay her three times what you count out each week. And it wouldn't be a bad thing. Especially not for Malinda, who could handle a store and the pharmacy with one hand tied behind her back. Mr. Gaddy could take his arthritic knees and china doll of a wife to the Florida sun.

I didn't plan to be a part of the Foodland crowd, but somehow the music drew me. I stood on the edge and listened as bass fiddles vibrated even the newly planted grass. The burlapped, balled and still-reeling-from-shock infant trees around the parking lot looked naked, a little startled to be here. The band stood on a platform in the middle of the parking lot. Red banners on poles blew in the breeze behind them. I saw someone approach the stage, a woman in an orange cape. Crazy Reba.

I caught my breath.

The bandleader in a red-checked shirt, white jeans and cowboy hat leaned over to listen to something Crazy Reba said. He held the bow to his fiddle out like a baton and shook his head. She persisted. He kept shaking his head. Finally he nodded with a frown and she climbed the steps and stood beside him on the stage looking like a meek and mild orphan child.

When the last note of "Rocky Top" floated toward the highest cloud, the leader held up his hand and his bow. "Folks, we got a request from this lady." He motioned to Crazy Reba. "She wants to sing a song she hasn't heard in a long time. Folks, there were tears in her eyes when she said it, and folks, I can stand of lot of things, but I can't stand to see a lady cry."

With that Reba lifted up her face, all her jewelry shining in the sun, and sang in a clear, child's voice, "Jesus loves me, this I know, for the Bible tells me so."

The crowd buzzed for a minute, then quieted until Reba finished and stepped down. There was an awkward silence. No one knew whether to applaud or not. Finally Reba started applauding herself and everyone joined in.

I walked home feeling something lifted from my life. Not a lead weight quite, but at least a little bundle of worries aside and out of my way. One piece of the puzzle clicked in place. Miss Lavinia's jewelry had been found. Now to fit it to the others.

Scott was about to apply the last coat of the varnish on top of the last pineapple stencil when I stopped by the sunporch. "Beautiful," I said. "It looks perfect." With the ruffled valances up, the tablecloths on and little bud vases with sprigs of whatever happened to be blooming in the yard . . . the place would look inviting, charming and cozy. Plus the food would do Mama Alice proud. I would see to that. Now that the painting was finished, I could design menus and plan an opening ad for the newspaper. I wanted a border print that included pineapples for the menus and my ad. I planned to always offer Mama Alice's pineapple muffins on the menu. They would be the House Special.

"A couple coats of polymer ought to hold it several years, I'd think," Scott said. He rocked back on his heels and surveyed his work.

"Wonderful," I said.

"Assuming of course you don't have a constant stream of heavy foot traffic, standing room only and things like that."

"I'd love to have things like that," I said. "They would spell success. Sweet-smelling success. But I'm realistic. And this is Littleboro, not Pinehurst. I'll take ten to twenty a day and be happy. Very happy."

I made us both iced coffee, sat on a stool at the counter and pored over Mama Alice's old cookbooks. Some of the pages were spattered, tan and torn. I turned each loose leaf of the notebook carefully and smiled over some of the names and notes. "Miss Wanema Kratt's Blue Cheese Dressing. Add a tablespoon more milk. Wanema always did make things a tad too dry." Or "The Salad Mildred Mottsinger Made for Her Daughter's Wedding Brunch" and "Herbert Clark's Basting for Birds." The cookbook was like the story of Mama Alice's life.

In the back were recipes on index cards, recipes clipped from newspapers and magazines. I flipped through them and made mental notes to go through them more carefully later and decide which ones to file or discard. Several slips of paper slid to my lap and some fell to the floor. I picked them up, started to go through them, then stopped. Here was a recipe in the same handwriting as the threatening note I had gotten. The note that said Mama Alice was pushed. I turned over the speckled page to the back. It was blank. There was no name on the recipe, but the same bold, upright letters had written of death and threats . . . and Scalloped Tomatoes.

CHAPTER FIFTEEN

I stood on my front walk holding *The Mess.*
It carried no national news. Those few in
Littleboro who wanted to know what went
on in the "real" world had to go to the
drugstore for the Raleigh *News & Observer*
or subscribe. Most people read *The Pilot*
religiously, had read it all their lives. It was
the gospel.

Still in my robe and slippers, hair un-
combed, I didn't think anyone would be out
so early. But there was Verna. Verna who
seemed to know everything that happened
in Littleboro any hour of the day or night.
Plus the details.

Verna had Robert Redford on his red
leather leash. "He goes crazy over oxalis
this time of year," she whispered. Her
breath smelled like the inside of a rusty
leather trunk. Robert Redford flicked an
ear as if he'd heard her. "I swear," Verna
said, "he knows when I'm talking about

him. That rabbit."

I unrolled my paper, glanced at headlines announcing "Big Crowds Expected at May Fair" and "Big Crowds Attend Foodland Opening." Big crowds in Littleboro were fifty or more.

The Mess had reprinted an article from the *News & Observer* about the remodeling of an older home. This one had the country motif coming out its walls. It was too cute for words. Why did people think they had to "country" up an older house? Every house has its own personality, I thought. I resolved that the Dixie Dew would not display one single lace-trimmed wooden heart that said "Welcome" or "Back Door Friends Are Best" or "Home Is Where You Hang Your Heart." The one thing I did know about an older home was that everything costs twice what you estimate and takes twice as long as you think.

Verna said, "You know that Debbie Dellinger, Father Roderick's housekeeper? Seems she and her sidekick boyfriend were arrested at Rider's Ridge in South Carolina. I've heard tell that flea market is so big, you can walk all day and still not see it all."

Robert Redford lifted a hind foot, scratched himself.

"Smart," said Verna. "I never would have

given that woman credit for having that much sense. Who at a flea market is going to ask where anything came from? Who cares? All they want is something for nothing. And that's what she got." Verna laughed at her own joke. "Something for nothing but some nerve and a little bit of effort. It's the biggest flea market in the South, must be a real hellhole."

"For her at least." I almost laughed. Verna surprised me using that language. It was definitely not little-old-lady language.

"Did they recover all of it?" I asked. I remembered there had been some lovely furniture in the parish house, a number of antiques. The housekeeper had cleaned out everything but dust balls under the beds.

"The church will get the money she made from it," Verna said, "I'm sure. All she's got on her, but what good will that do? Probably most of the stuff was practically given away. She got a fraction of what it was worth." Verna picked up Robert Redford, scratched behind his ears.

"Wonder how *The Mess* will play it?" Verna continued. "Big photo on page one of Ossie DelGardo with the handcuffed housekeeper and some caption that reads like the most wanted, most dangerous, worst criminal in fifty states has just been apprehended here in Littleboro, or an inch paragraph under the obituaries back of page one? Depends on how who's who in the church wants it played . . . loud and dramatic, wringing scandal for all it's worth, and sympathy, or as quickly skipped over and quietly forgotten as possible? It will be interesting to see."

I flipped through *The Mess.* There was no mention of Mrs. Housekeeper and her midnight raid. That would either make headlines next issue, as Verna said, or get an inch mention buried on an inside page.

"And that cousin," Verna said, "Lester Moore. He's been hanging around this town like he's ready to pounce on something that belongs to him. I don't know what could. Who'd ever heard of him before Lavinia died? He could be fake for all I know. How do we know he's who he says he is?" She looked up the street toward the courthouse. "Ossie DelGardo'd haul in his own mother if he had half a notion." Verna had an inch-long safety pin where a button had been at the top of her brown cotton dress. Her slip hung out, a very dirty slip, almost the color of her dress.

And I worried someone would see me in my robe, I thought. That worry was the voice of Mama Alice from childhood. The

181

one that never wore pins in her underwear. "What if there'd be an accident and you'd have to go to the hospital? Why, somebody'd see your underwear."

Verna hurried home with the rabbit in her arms, leash dragging behind them like a skinny red rat tail.

I thought of the housekeeper later when I walked to the post office. It was almost funny to think of her and her boyfriend backing a U-Rental up to a house and helping themselves, then heading for a flea market to unload it. Resourceful. Was their gripe with the church, Father Roderick or the world in general? What was their story? But most important, were they the ones to kill Father Roderick? And Miss Lavinia? After all, Father Roderick had been the one to return Miss Lavinia's handbag. The two connected somewhere, sometime, and now both were dead.

I flipped through my magazines, flyers and bills, almost bumped Rosalie Jones, Malinda's mother, who had the baby, Elvis, in a stroller. "You're the stuff." I bent to talk to him and kissed the top of his head. He smelled like sweet potatoes. "And I hear your grandma's spoiling you rotten."

Rosalie laughed. "I know who spread that rumor. The one I learned on."

The baby had Malinda's bright eyes and wide smile. I squeaked his blue toy dog and he squealed in delight as if I had squeezed him a hug.

"Malinda's home sprawled out on the couch with some old high school stuff spread out around her. I hope she's going through it to clean out, throw away . . . my house is a rat's nest. I told her it was a crime and a disgrace to stay inside on a day like this." Rosalie shook her head. "I don't think she even heard me. Give that girl a book and the world could blow up. She wouldn't know it."

Rosalie wheeled off down the street. Elvis waved "bye-bye."

Lester Moore, Miss Lavinia's cousin, stood on the courthouse steps, head bent, deep in conversation with Ethan Drummond. Sometimes I wondered how much business ever went on in offices. Moore cut his eyes at me. He touched his forehead in greeting and smiled halfway. A smile that said, I can eat you up and spit out your bones and no one will be the wiser.

I shook off his look that felt like arrows aimed at my back, tried to walk like I hadn't seen a thing and shuffle through my mail at the same time. There was the electric bill and a newsletter from an organization of art teachers announcing the annual meeting in San Francisco. They'll have to meet without me, I thought. An envelope said I was the million-dollar winner of the house of my dreams. I laughed at that one. The house of my dreams stood in front of me and it could gulp money down like a dragon ate pearls.

The fourth envelope made me stop in the middle of the walk. There was that handwriting again. The same bold slant and black ink handwriting that had written "Mama Alice was pushed" was here in my hand. I sat on the stack of bricks and held the letter addressed to some genealogical organization in New York City, a letter stamped with the pointing purple hand that read: "Undeliverable. Return to Sender." And there in the top left-hand corner was the sender, the sender's address, and the person who had threatened my life. The person who knew how Mama Alice died and perhaps even caused it. It read: "Verna Crowell, 333 N. Main Street, Littleboro, NC." Her mail had gotten in with mine.

Now I had no doubt, but what to do about it? Confront Verna? What if she denied it? And why had she written the note? What did she know? And what didn't she want me to know?

Or had the note been a tip to set me off

on a quest to find out the truth of my grandmother's death?

Friday morning the Puttermans left full of orange cinnamon French toast topped with my special strawberry sauce.

"I'm tempted to stay one more night," Leon said. "Just to get another bite of that barbecue. It was the finest kind. The finest kind."

Ida Plum and I changed beds, cleaned the baths, vacuumed and dusted. As a team we were done in fifty minutes flat. "Back in business," Ida Plum said as she wound the cord. "And none the worse for wear."

"Speak for yourself," I said. I put lavender soaps in the baths, on the closet shelves and in the drawers and left the doors slightly ajar.

Scott didn't come until after lunch, but we painted woodwork on the sunporch until almost five. "Pepto-Bismol pink," he said.

I ignored him.

"The Pink Panther rides again," he said.

I kept painting.

"When I close my eyes tonight, I will have only pink dreams," he said, "but it could be worse."

"Paint," I said. "Just paint. We are not gearing up to get a spot in *Our State* magazine." Truth was, his banter lifted my spirits and I hummed as I painted. The tearoom was becoming a tearoom. It was going to look glorious.

As I painted I thought of the broken half of Reba's earring that Sherman had found and I had mistaken for a lizard. It had lain all night on the desk blotter. "I bet that earring is real," I said. "Knowing Reba, she wore it on her underwear."

"Reba never does anything halfway," Scott said.

"I think it is the real stuff and Reba, Miss Lavinia and Father Roderick are all connected. She's in and out of every nook and cranny in this town. I don't think she'd hurt anyone, nor actually steal anything, but if that jewelry is real and she was wearing it around, she could be in danger."

"I know," Scott said. "This town is not your all-American red, white and blue, Fourth of July, Norman Rockwell painting of a place these days."

"Okay," I told him when we stopped to have a glass of iced tea. "The answer to the question lies with the wizard."

"On Main Street." Scott raised his glass.

"Raynard Bennett."

"He never struck me as a wizard at anything but passing the collection plate on

Sunday mornings," Scott said.

"That's right," I said. "He does always look and act like the perfect usher. But he knows his jewelry. He probably teethed on it."

I changed from jeans into a wraparound denim skirt. As surely as I went out in jeans and scarf, my hair in disarray, I would run into half the town. Not that it mattered, but Mama and Mama Alice always said, "Keep yourself clean. You never know who you'll meet."

I slid the half earring into the breast pocket on my blouse. "See you." I gave Scott a cheery little parade queen wave of my hand.

The air smelled like lilacs. It almost seemed a pale purple. I thought how many thousand times I had walked this sidewalk. I knew every dip, crack and irregular corner. I knew the wisteria on the Britts' fence. Another house going to slow ruin. Wisteria hid a lot of latticework that had not been painted in years. It was probably only a step away from toothpicks for termites.

The old movie theater was now the meeting place of The Fellowship for Power, Peace and Plenty. On Sunday mornings and Wednesday nights, fifteen or twenty cars parked along the street in front. I knew the four established steeples of First Presbyterian, First Baptist, First Methodist and St. Ann's looked down on such an assembly . . . not that any of that congregation would ever grace their doors.

In the window of Faye's Fashionette I glanced at a patterned skirt spread out like an umbrella beneath a wicker table. The matching blouse hung flat as a skeleton on a white wicker screen behind.

When I passed the drugstore, Malinda rounded the corner. She almost bumped into me. "This kind of day, I'd rather be anywhere than behind that counter," she said. "I got spring fever all over."

"I know," I said. "Even the air makes me feel light-headed. Your mama said you were sprawled out on the couch looking at old high school stuff."

"That was then; this is now," Malinda said. "I was looking for something. Come in for a Coke." She held the drugstore door open.

"Will do on my way home!" I called, and turned the corner to Bennett's Jewelry.

As a child, I thought all the wealth in the world was in the windows of Bennett's Jewelry. Black velvet drapes and swags and folds held rings and pins and bracelets, watches and crystal vases, the thinnest china and cut-glass goblets. I used to stand there and mentally buy things to take home to Mama Alice. My graduation watch had come from Bennett's and the birthstone ring for my tenth birthday. The ring I lost in Lemon Lake on a picnic two weeks later. I never trusted myself with "real" jewelry since. Not that I had funds to invest in any. Jewelry was too easy to lose or have stolen.

Raynard Bennett put his jeweler's lens in after he took the half earring from me. He turned it over several times, studied it, polished it with a cloth, then studied it more. "Your mama's or Miss Alice's?"

"Neither," I said.

"Old enough to be," Raynard said. "And worth a pretty penny. If you got the rest of it. Or even if you haven't."

He put a clear liquid on a cloth and rubbed, his long fingers steady and knowing. "Diamonds have always been a girl's best friend."

"Diamonds?" I said. "But I thought —"

"It's gold with little winks of emeralds in between."

"Oh," I said, "but —"

Raynard put the earring in a case and snapped it shut. "A pair of those would run over five thousand."

"Dollars?"

"Maybe a little more." Raynard put the case in his palm and held it toward me. "We can remount for you. Or sell."

"No," I said. My hand trembled as I took the half earring. "Not now." I slid it in the pocket of my skirt next to a piece of paper. Probably some old shopping list left from Lord knows when. I thanked Raynard and hurried out. Real diamonds. I had a half an earring worth a lot of money. How much was the rest of the stuff I'd stashed in Ethan Drummond's office worth? No wonder that cousin of Miss Lavinia's had been in such a tizzy to get his hands on the stuff. Oh, Reba, I thought, do you know what you've gotten yourself into? Of course she didn't. She couldn't.

I was almost past the drugstore when I remembered Malinda. I'd just pop in and tell her we would make it another time. I felt too muddled for conversation.

"Inventory," Malinda said. "I'm ready for a break." She put her pencil behind her ear, popped her clipboard down and came around front. I felt the jewelry case bulge conspicuously.

Malinda waved me to a seat. "This is my treat." She scooped ice, ran Cokes and stirred. She winked at Mrs. Gaddy, who was scraping the grill. "One of my many perks."

"Perk away," Mrs. Gaddy said. "You and me both."

"I'm glad you asked me. I needed a break," I said.

"Give this peace another twenty minutes." Malinda leaned back in her chair. "Then all hell breaks loose."

"That hasn't changed," I said. Schoolkids still poured in hungry, loud and thirsty. But most of all, loud.

"I don't miss it." Malinda laughed. "Being that age. Do you?"

"I don't think about it," I said. "Unless I've scraped paint for a couple of hours, peeled wallpaper or hand sanded floors . . . then I feel something I never felt at seventeen. Tired."

"How's the house coming?"

"Slowly, slowly," I said. "I'd say it's about half where I want it to be."

"I admire your spunk," Malinda said.

"Spunk is the offspring of necessity," I said.

"All this admiration isn't why I invited you in. Not that I didn't want to see you anyway . . . but I'm worried about something. Ossie DelGardo's asking questions about you around town."

"Me?" I said. "That man's despicable. More than that. He's like something slink-

191

ing around town. Some animal that crawled out of the pond some moonlit night."

"I know. I know," Malinda said. "He has all the personality of a weasel. But that's not the point here. He's found out the poison that killed Miss Lavinia Lovingood was a type of hemlock."

"Hemlock. That what Socrates drank. Wasn't it? Hemlock?"

"And others," Malinda said. "But Miss Lavinia is the only one we know. The question is . . . where did it come from and more than that . . . who gave it to her?"

"My God," I said. "He doesn't think I had anything to do with poisoning her . . . does he? What would I get out of it?"

"Just thought I'd tell you," Malinda said. She finished her Coke with a swirl of her straw in the ice and one last attempt to get any in the bottom of the glass. "As bad as I hate to, the tea party's over and I've got to get back to work."

"Thanks," I said.

"Take care." Malinda headed toward the back of the store. "Don't do anything I wouldn't!" she called.

"Trust me," I said. "I won't."

I somehow managed to get out the door and halfway home before my temper got really boiling. If I were a kettle, I'd be whistling like hell. I felt that steamed. More than steamed, damn mad. Who does Ossie DelGardo think he is? The FBI? CBS? CIA? UDC? The more initials I named the funnier it got, and I started laughing in spite of myself. The whole thing was ridiculous. Stupid and senseless and . . . well, a lot of things I didn't know but was going to find out. If Ossie DelGardo wanted to watch my every move, he owed me some answers to some questions. At least that. Damn him.

Scott had gone home when I got back to the Dixie Dew. Or somewhere. His truck was not in the driveway. I wanted him to be there. I needed a sounding board. I needed an ear and somehow I didn't think Ida Plum was someone who would take much of my screeching.

I got the mail from the box and flipped through it; envelopes marked "Occupant" or magazines that wanted me to try them free for the first month. There was nothing that looked like a reservation.

When I pulled the jewelry box from my pocket the piece of paper I'd felt earlier came with it. How long had it been since I'd worn this skirt? I unfolded the paper and read: "The grave is a fine and very cozy place, didn't you think?" The note was written in the same black ink and with the same slanted thin strokes of handwriting as the first note. The note that said Mama Alice was pushed. I dropped the note on the walk. I felt like screaming as if something had bitten me. Evil. It reeked of evil. This town reeked of evil as if it sat under a poison cloud and the creeks and streams ran with it.

CHAPTER SIXTEEN

Bricks from the low wall pricked the backs of my legs like fear. I had taken the first available seat and now just sat holding my mail and Verna's returned letter. A flock of robins swooped to the lawn where the condominiums were under construction. The birds rustled leaves in the magnolia trees. A car went by. I saw and heard, but it all blurred and one black thought kept beating in my head: Verna was mixed up in a murder. Make that two murders. Almost three. What could I do?

Take the nasty threatening little notes I'd received, and the letter, over to Ossie Del-Gardo, slap them on his desk and say, "I've found your killer." The notes didn't say Verna was a killer, but they might point the way to one. Ossie DelGardo would laugh me and the letter out of his pale green, pine-scented office. He would tell me to go tend my muffin making at the Dixie Dew. Isn't that what B and Bs were all about? Renting out spare rooms and calling it a business? And murdering guests as they slept, robbing them of their last possessions? That was how Ossie DelGardo saw me. I was on page 1 in his book of suspects. In fact, the only one, until Father Roderick's housekeeper cleaned out the rectory. That ought to put her somewhere in the running with me. Tied for first place at least.

I let myself in the front door and heard ripping and splitting sounds from the rear of the house. It sounded like somebody was tearing all hell out of something. "Scott!" I called.

"Yo!" he called from the kitchen where he stood on a stool, held a crowbar and pulled cabinets loose from the wall. "Ida Plum stacked the stuff from this cabinet in the pantry so I could start here. I couldn't stand to see you making do in this monstrosity of a kitchen anymore. I'm taking it wall by wall."

"I thought you were gone," I said. "Your truck —"

"Around back. So I don't have to haul these babies so far."

I could have hugged his bare back. Put my arm around his shoulders, pulled him close and just cried. Because he cared.

Because I was scared. Because I just plain didn't know what to do, where to go from here . . . all of it.

"One wall at a time," he said. "That's how we'll take it. You've got these drawn off . . . drawers and shelves and all those good things where you want them. I'll do the rest."

"But the money . . ." I started.

"What's a charge account for, if not to charge?" He worked nails from a piece of molding. "Solid pine. You don't find wood this good these days. I'll reuse all I can."

I stared at the stack of splintered boards at his feet.

"Okay, so some of it goes to the fireplace, but think how toasty your toes are going to be next winter. I've started a stack in the garage for you alone."

"Can you take a break?" I asked, and held up his empty coffee cup. "I can make a fresh pot. I need to talk."

"Let me get this last cabinet down and I'll give you my undivided attention."

Carefully I laid the letters on the table, started coffee and pulled carrot pecan muffins from the freezer. I had no new reservations for overnight guests at the Dixie Dew. One did not pay off renovations without income with which to do so. Unless windfalls landed in one's lap, and Miss Lavinia's jewelry didn't count. That's not gains, ill-gotten or otherwise. The jewelry was part of her estate that Mr. Green Polyester Pants Cousin, Lester Moore, would probably get his pinkies on with glee. At least Crazy Reba was out of danger, roaming around town with plastic rings and things from her fingers to her toes, buzzing like a June bug.

Scott stirred sugar and milk in his coffee and took a long, satisfying drink. "That's what I needed. Real coffee."

"And I need real help," I said.

"Shoot." Scott reached over and covered my hand with his rough and tender one.

"I'm into something and I don't know the way out," I said.

"Road maps free of charge . . . name your destination."

"I know who's been leaving those notes."

He waited.

I shoved Verna's returned letter toward him, then unfolded the notes I'd received over the last few days.

Scott studied them, then let out a little whistle. "Not old Verna. Not Miss Priss and Proper. Goody Blue Hair?"

"It can't be anybody else."

"So, do you invite her for tea and serve these?"

"I hadn't thought about it, but that's an idea. She's got to be confronted. She's got to know that I know she's mixed up in these murders."

"What then?" Scott put his empty cup in the dishwasher.

"I don't know. I'll take it one step at a time. Like your cabinets, one section at a time."

"Meanwhile, it's Can you come to tea, Verna C.?"

"Yes," I said. "I'll bake Littleboro's Cream Cheese Pound Cake. She can't refuse."

"Feed your enemies," Scott said, "and they'll follow you everywhere."

"Verna isn't an enemy. I may be into something bigger than I can handle. I can't . . . I won't believe she had anything to do with murder."

"Just don't go for tea at her house, my sweet." He laid a hand lightly on my shoulder. "Promise me."

"Don't worry," I said. "This is my party. And it's going to stay that way."

CHAPTER SEVENTEEN

At three o'clock I took the pound cake, all golden brown and crusted on top, from the oven. It filled the kitchen with vanilla and sugar and a hundred days of my childhood. I could have cried if I let myself.

Scott had cleared the kitchen of excess boards. Verna was due at four, and when the doorbell rang I thought at first it was Verna coming early. I almost panicked. Scott had hung a green-striped sheet over the entrance to the pantry. We'd shoved everything from the cupboard into it. When the kitchen was completed the pantry was going to be an office for me, a place to keep Mama Alice's collection of cookbooks and the B-and-B records, to plan menus, to shut the door on the world.

"I'm hanging around for this," Scott said. "No matter what you say."

"Did I say anything?" I asked on my way to the hall.

I was relieved to see through the glass the outlines of two people. Just don't let them be Ossie DelGardo or Lester Moore, I thought. Those two I can do without any day of the week. I opened the door.

"Are you open?" a woman in purple slacks asked. "We were driving through and saw your sign, so I said, 'Harry, let's check. It won't hurt to check.'"

"Here we are," Harry said with an apologetic little slice of a smile.

"Of course," I said. I'd forgotten I also ran a bed-and-breakfast. "Come in." I opened the door, took them to my registration desk. "If you'd like to see the rooms first . . ." I said, indicating the stairs, "you've got first choice."

The woman went upstairs while Harry registered them. Mr. and Mrs. A. Harry Harlton of Elmsville, NY. "On our way to Florida," he said. "Her sister lives there and we go this way twice a year. Usually stay in a motel, but we came to this first and Louise likes to try new things. I'm not much for that myself. All I want is a hard bed and a hot shower."

I laughed. "Then you want the Periwinkle Room. That has the firmest mattress."

"Back trouble." Harry rubbed his lower back. "Had it all my life, and Father before me. 'The Harlton back,' we say, when it acts up."

"There's parking in the rear," I said as Harry Harlton went out for their luggage.

Now I wasn't alone in the house to deal with Verna, but how could you discuss something this serious with some stranger poking his head in to ask where one would find an extra lightbulb, to say the lamp wasn't working . . . or some such situation?

Louise Harlton called from the top of the stairs, "Put us down for the blue room. I think that bed's better for Harry!"

"Breakfast is anytime before ten," I told her. "Let me know if you need anything."

"Will do." Harry Harlton took an overnight bag and cosmetic case upstairs. "Any place we can get a decent steak around here?"

"Floyd's," I said. "On Main Street. If you don't mind hush puppies on your plate along with the baked potatoes. Tell him I sent you."

That took care of the Harltons for dinner . . . and getting them out of the house for a while. Maybe Verna would be late. Very late.

I lifted the paper doily from atop the cake where I'd sprinkled powdered sugar. Ha. What if I'd sprinkled it with roach poison instead? Would Verna know the difference? I had read somewhere that aging caused people's taste buds to dull, lose sensation. Is that what happened to Miss Lavinia and whatever poisonous thing she'd eaten that killed her? Whatever it was, wasn't in this house, I thought. Verna better have some answers.

"I'm Sheetrocking this wall," Scott said in the kitchen, "and when I'm not hammering I can hear everything being said."

"Thanks," I said as the phone rang. "And this is only powdered sugar . . . even if the thought is otherwise." I was ashamed of myself. Verna was an old lady. She didn't want to hurt anyone . . . ever. Not unless she had to.

"Honey," Verna said when I picked up the phone, "can we make that dessert? I got into cleaning a closet and I never saw so much stuff in my life. That's what this weather does to me. It'll kill me yet . . . before I'm through . . . if this cleaning spell don't let up."

"Seven?" I asked, and Verna hung up.

It was seven thirty when Verna came in. "That darn rabbit. When he knows I'm in a hurry, he's slow as constipation."

Any other time I would have laughed. Tonight I almost dropped the cups and saucers. In fact, the cups rattling in the saucers sounded exactly how I felt inside . . . shaky, my thoughts clattering together.

"Decaf?" Verna asked. "I hope that's decaf." She pulled out a kitchen chair, waved a finger to Scott and leaned over the pound cake. "You did Miss Alice proud, honey. I bet you couldn't count how many pound cakes that woman made in her lifetime, and never a one that wasn't smooth and creamy enough to melt in your mouth."

"Let's take our coffee out to the sunporch," said I. "I want you to see my stenciling."

Verna poured her cup half full of cream, then let me fill the rest with coffee. "I like a little coffee in my cream." Verna laughed. "That's what Calbert always said."

I put cake on plates, carried them on a tray and the coffee out to the sunporch.

"Why, it's just sweet as can be," Verna said when she stepped onto the sunporch. "Who in the world but you would have ever thought about painting this old floor? You can hardly tell it's paint . . . it shines so."

We talked of the bed-and-breakfast, the tearoom. I held up swags of fabric I'd bought for the windows and tablecloths.

"Cute," Verna said, and clapped her hands. "Just cute as can be. I never thought you

204

could do so much with paint and draping some cloth around."

I waited until Verna finished her cake down to the last crumb and sat sipping on her second cup of coffee. Then I pulled out the notes, unfolded them.

Verna's eyes grew wide and she choked a little, started to cough. Then she cried. She crumpled and uncrumpled the embroidered napkin, and fat, hot tears big as marbles rolled down her dry old creviced cheeks.

I waited again.

Verna took off her glasses, wiped them with the napkin, then blew her nose.

I winced, still said nothing, but reached behind me in the kitchen for a whole box of tissues and handed them to Verna.

"You weren't afraid, were you?" Verna said at last.

"Wouldn't you be?"

Verna looked up, her triangle of a chin quivering.

"They were threats," I said. "And notes that said my grandmother was murdered. Did you push her?"

"Lord, Lord, I . . ." Verna's eyes filled again. "You know better than that. I'd never lift a finger to hurt your grandmother. We'd been friends sixty years."

"Then why the notes?"

"I can't talk about it." Verna sniffed.

"You did write them. You don't deny that," I said.

"I can't talk about it." Verna looked away, and the hairy mole on her cheek wiggled as if it wanted to crawl off, go somewhere on its own.

"I think you'd better." I was surprised I could make my voice so firm, unwavering.

"I can't," Verna said, and choked a little.

"If you can't, who can?" I decided Verna would not leave this house until I had some answers. Some names to put with some deeds.

"You can't make me." Verna played with the tissues in her lap.

She sounded like a child. Is her mind going? I wondered. Please not now. Don't let her click out on me. "You can tell me," I almost whispered. "I promise I won't tell anyone."

"Cross your heart? Hope to die?" Verna asked.

"Well, no," I said. "You can trust me without that, can't you?"

Verna pushed her hair back from her face with both hands, then leaned forward. " 'I'm nobody!' " Her eyes were bright as feathers.

"Nobody?"

" 'Who are you?' " her eyes looked blank. Was anybody still in there?

" 'Don't tell,' " she said. " 'They'd banish us, you know.' "

Emily Dickinson. She's quoting Emily Dickinson to me. Once an English major, always an English major.

"Who is Nobody?" I asked as gently as I could, reached over to touch Verna on her arm. Bring her back to base maybe?

"Tempie's house is falling down, falling down, falling down," Verna began to sing. "My fair Lavinia." She hiccupped, put her hand over her mouth and giggled.

"What's Miss Lavinia got to do with all this?" I asked.

"Why, everything," Verna said, suddenly lucid. "I got so excited when I heard she was coming back. I wrote her right away and said come for lunch. Not Tempie, just me and Lavinia. Tempie was always so jealous, she'd just snip and snap every time she got around Lavinia."

I poured Verna more coffee. Let her keep talking. Truth had to be in there somewhere. Now she seemed sobering up, landing back down from whatever realm she'd spun into when I started probing.

"Tempie always wanted what Lavinia had. She wanted what anybody else had. When your granddaddy married Miss Alice, Tempie threw a fit. Lavinia and I had a little party for her. We just knew Tempie wouldn't come, but she did, and you know what?"

"What?" I asked, though the last thing I wanted to hear was some social slight of fifty years ago. But the old Verna was back and I was listening.

"You know what Tempie gave Margaret Alice at her bridal shower? Scissors," Verna said. "And not even a coin with them to cut the bad luck. Lavinia and I gave her silver. We said that was something she could always use."

Let her run to the end of her thread, I thought. Maybe some of it will connect.

"Tempie didn't want Lavinia to come here," Verna whispered, and looked behind her. The night stood navy blue and close against the windows.

"Why?" I asked.

"Father Roderick, that's why. He'd find out and Tempie would be up the creek. Up the creek." Verna giggled.

She's had something to drink, I thought. Sherry. I knew Mama Alice had said something before about Verna and her "daily tipple." I'd thought several times in the evenings Verna acted giggly. Tonight, she'd had several sherries.

"She said Robert Redford would disappear." Verna suddenly got serious. "She said I'd never know what happened to him." Verna's shoulder shook a little and she looked behind her again.

"Did she lock him in the mausoleum?" With me? I started to add. "Was that Tempie?"

"It wasn't her," Verna said. "Tempie wouldn't do it. She loves animals. She goes to Harold's grave every day."

"Who did?"

Verna ignored her question. "Tempie said I'd never see Robert Redford again, but I did." Verna looked quickly at me. "I didn't know you'd be there. You found him."

Who? I wanted to ask. Who was she protecting? I wanted to take Verna by the shoulders and shake the answers out. The notes had been harmless. Verna hadn't done anything except scare me, give me some sleepless nights.

Verna sat with her eyes closed, head down now. She shredded tissue in her lap like she was making a nest for a mouse. "I'm tired. It's late and I'm tired. I don't want to play bridge anymore."

"Okay," I said. "We'll talk tomorrow."

Verna left by the back door, wobbling along the path between the magnolias. I watched her lilting walk, almost felt like going after her, offering to help her to her back door. Then I remembered Verna had written those notes. I just didn't know why. She might be old and frail, I thought, but she's not entirely innocent. I watched from the porch until Verna was safely inside her own house and the porch light snapped off.

Had I really accomplished anything? I asked myself as I straightened the sunporch. Not much except I didn't think I'd be finding any more notes. At least not anytime soon. There was something going on between Verna and Tempie. How long had it been going on and had my grandmother been caught in it?

"You heard," I said as Scott came in the kitchen.

"Most of it," he said. "And I feel better about the notes. Just don't forget there were two murders in this town last week. One of them was in this house."

"I don't need you to stay, if that's what you're saying," I said. "I've guests. And I've good locks and this is still Littleboro."

"But not the Littleboro you knew," he reminded me, checking the lock on the front door and turning off the porch light. "And you can't blame a guy for giving it a shot."

He grinned. Those blue eyes almost got to me.

"Go," I said. Those blue eyes and that little smile pulled at me.

"Not fair. Haven't I been the model of decency? Haven't I gone beyond mere mortal limitations in trying to undo the besmirched reputation of my grand gender?"

"Go," I said again, and opened the back door. His truck gleamed in the side driveway. "Your trusty steed awaits. It needs you."

"It needs gas," he said. "And I need a whole new day to begin again the unending job of restoring this white elephant of a house for my lovely but penniless employer." His tone was mocking, but inlaid with a hint of seriousness.

"I need time to think and you're not helping," I said.

"Will this help?" He kissed me lightly and quickly. "Good night!" he called softly, and left before I could say anything.

I locked the door behind him. I was too tired to think beyond how much I needed a sound night's sleep.

CHAPTER EIGHTEEN

Before I went to bed, I set up the sideboard with the food warmers and fixed the coffee so all I had to do in the morning was flip the switch. I put place mats out, pinched faded flowers and dead leaves from the arrangement on the sideboard. Even then, after I dimmed the lights and stood back, I decided it still looked frayed and sad. Like I felt.

There are no rules against picking flowers at 10:00 P.M., I said to myself as I took Mama Alice's old cutting scissors off the nail in the pantry, turned on the porch light and trekked to the yard. Besides, anything cut this late in the day was already dew drenched and would probably stay fresh indoors longer.

I cut roses and some tall spikes from the lilac tree. I loved to mix pinks, reds and purples. The colors vibrated and gave off energy. I needed that.

The neighborhood was quiet. A dog barked somewhere over in Queentown, the streetlights glowed and not even a car passed to break the silence. The air smelled of decayed lilacs and honeysuckle. Real spring was being brief; summer was coming in heavy with honeysuckle. I wanted to stay outside longer, to sit on the porch and just rock awhile.

All was dark at Verna's. Not a light burned. "Let her sleep it off," I said. "I'm not through with her. Verna Crowell has answers and I'm going to get them if I have to pour out all her sherry and force black coffee down her gullet like stuffing a turkey."

Before I went in, I snipped a few sprigs of parsley from the bed Mama Alice always grew by the back door. I'd use it to garnish the scrambled eggs in the morning.

I ran water over the parsley, turned it over and sprayed the back. In the dark, I had also cut a weed of some sort. I pulled the weed out, examined it closely. Funny, I thought, how some plants look a lot alike, cousins in the same family. We eat parsley. I held the weed up, spread its leaves. It looked like parsley, I thought, but the stem was too thick, the leaves not pointed on the ends, and it wasn't curly at all. Nobody has probably ever tasted this homely fellow or would want to, this country cousin. I wasn't about to taste it. Mr. Booth, my high school biology teacher who ate, slept and breathed botany, always said don't put anything in your mouth you can't identify first. And then only if you're 110 percent sure it's safe. He told them how some garden club president somewhere had used a wild plant that looked like parsley on a sandwich tray and if anyone had eaten it they would have died on the spot. "Lucky for that garden club," he'd said, "nobody ever ate the parsley."

"Nobody?" I asked. One reason this parsley bed grew so well was that not only did it have a sunny and protected spot near the back door, but it was actively pruned and it stayed green and growing most of the year.

I put the parsley in a plastic bag in the refrigerator, yawned and turned off the lights, threw the lookalike weed in the trash.

I stood at the bottom of the stairs. The Harltons' light under their door was out. It had been out since soon after Verna left and Scott went home.

I closed my own bedroom door, then slid in the chain latch. I had put that on soon after opening the bed-and-breakfast. What if you hosted someone who sleepwalked? Or worse? Not likely, but it didn't hurt to be careful.

I was almost asleep when I remembered something about Mr. Booth's wild-parsley story and hemlock. The deadly cousin to parsley was called water hemlock. I remembered now where we'd keyed it on our field trip . . . the Merritt property. The memory didn't help me get to sleep, but when I did I dreamed of rabbits chased by poodles with red eyes and fangs. Poodles who wore jeweled collars and smiled as they danced on two legs. In the background Miss Tempie played and sang nude at a white grand piano. " 'Blest Be the Tie That Binds,' " she shrieked. The piano turned into some wheezy old pipe organ that blew up to a giant inflatable raft Verna sat on; then they floated down the river, organ, Miss Tempie and all. Verna kept giggling and waving like she was riding in a parade. Or was she crying and waving for help? I couldn't tell. The raft was moving fast, heading toward a bridge they couldn't go under. *Bump.* They bumped the bridge, the two women on the raft. I heard them bump and then I awoke. There was another bump. This one was real. Someone was in the house. My house.

I waited. It might be one of the Harltons up for a glass of milk. If so, they'd get it and go back upstairs. I listened for the stairs to sigh. My clock glowed 3:27. Then my doorknob rattled and there was the sound of my door knob turning, metal clicking, and the door opened.

The chain stopped it short and I sprang from the bed. "Who is it?" I called. "What do you want?"

No one answered. In the streetlight I saw thick fingers trying to work past the chain.

"Who is it?" I screamed again. This time I stood behind the door. I wanted to really scream, but my throat felt dry, raw and swollen shut.

The hand turned into a fist now and hammered at the chain. *Wham. Wham. Wham.*

I heard splinters. The screws were pulling loose. One more hard blow and the chain would be pulled from the wall.

A bulky, heavy body pushed hard at the door and the chain pulled and dangled. It was held only by a bit of stubborn wood.

I tried to push the door shut. My weight was nothing to what was on the other side. I screamed, and even to me my screams weren't loud enough. I sounded more shrill than serious.

"Help," I cried. "Someone, help."

Whoever was on the other side whammed the door again and I tried to think of something heavy to hit him with. Knock him out. There was no way I could push a chest of drawers in front of the door, and even if I could it would only delay, not stop, whoever wanted in my bedroom. Wanted me.

Any lamp I could reach would crumble like crackers in my hands. They were so old and fragile.

I whirled and in the light something gleamed on my drawing table. I snatched up the X-ACTO knife, held it as if my life depended on it and began to whack at the fingers. I jabbed as hard as I could and jabbed again. Again. Blood ran from the fingers that fumbled with the chain. I jabbed harder, then deeper. I felt the knife go in the flesh and I pulled. "I'll kill you!" I screamed. I kept screaming it, hysterically jabbing, frantic with the knife.

Wham. The wild bear of a creature pulled back his hand. I heard heavy footsteps, the *ting, ting, click* of metal as he walked, then only the sound of sweet silence.

I touched the chain. It was sticky with blood. My hand was covered with blood and shaking as I unlatched what was left of the hanging hook.

The hall was empty and the front door hung open. I ran, slammed and locked the door, then sagged against it and cried. I sank to the floor, my back still to the door, and just cried until I felt weak and emptied. As though I'd had a fever and it had drained all my strength.

I listened to any sounds from upstairs. Not even a snore. I remembered how Scott had said at one point all the doors at the Dixie Dew were solid wood. Not the modern doors of hollow cores. It was possible the Harltons hadn't heard a sound.

At the top of the stairs, the Harltons' door remained as closed as ever. Was it possible they heard nothing? Slept though my near murder, all my screams and whoever had banged and slammed against my door? Or had they heard everything and bolted themselves in? Too terrified to come out for even a peek?

The whole house was silent, sleeping. There seemed a peace in it. A false peace that could crack like an egg.

I trembled, stood in the hall in my rumpled, bloodstained nightgown and tried to decide what to do. Call Scott? Call Ida Plum?

Logic said call Ossie, report all this to Littleboro's finest. I knew in my heart of hearts that was what any sensible person would do, but I also knew in the back of my mind I'd be the laughingstock at the barbershop or Breakfast Nook for the next week, month, even talked about as part of Little-boro lore. It would be all over town that our little miss hostess with the mostess with her silly muffins and bed-and-breakfast had called Ossie in the middle of the night on some pretext. Even though I could show him the splintered door, my nightgown stains and all, he might figure I'd done it myself to get his attention. Like I was one of those single women who lived alone and were scared of their own shadow. Would imagine Peeping Toms who were only wish-ful thinking, anything to get a man in uniform poking around in their bushes at night.

In the bathroom, I watched the red bright-ness of blood stain the sink, then swirl down. I took a shower. I let the tub fill with hot water, then sat in it and soaked, think-ing of nothing but soap and hot water and steam and how good it felt. How good I felt to be warm and whole and alive. Oh, alive. Somehow I knew whoever it was wouldn't come back . . . not tonight.

I didn't feel as if I could ever sleep again, but in fresh pajamas and warm from my bath I fell across my bed and slept.

It was past seven when I woke to the sound of a key in the back door. I stiffened, listened, got ready to spring at or from whoever came through that door. For a minute it was last night all over again. I jumped from bed, dashed to hold my door shut, my hand on the blood-sticky chain latch, the other on my knife.

"Beth?" Scott called from the hall. "What the hell happened here last night?

I tore from my room.

Scott grabbed and held me. "My God, this looks like blood." He wiped at it with his finger. "Is this blood?"

I felt the warmth of his body seeping into mine and held back my tears.

I glanced toward the front door.

Scott followed my look. "The blood goes that way and back here . . . toward this room. Are you okay?" He held me apart from him, looked closely at me, then wrapped his arms around me.

He felt so good. Solid and good. "Someone broke in, tried to come in my bedroom. . . . I . . . I . . ." I couldn't stop stuttering.

He rubbed my arms briskly, my back, wrapped himself around me again.

"I'm okay," I finally said, and pulled reluctantly away. "But whoever it was is going to have one sore hand for a while." I showed Scott the stained X-ACTO knife.

Scott let out a whistle. "If this is what you do to gentlemen callers, remind me not to come unless I'm invited."

At breakfast I casually asked the Harltons how they slept.

"Why, honey," Louise Harlton said, "I slept like a log. I tell you I put those earplugs in and I go nighty-night."

"Earplugs?" I asked.

Harry Harlton blushed.

"He snores like a steam engine," said his wife. "I tried separate bedrooms for a while. And even that didn't work. He shakes the house. I have truly thought seriously about divorce."

"No, you didn't," her husband said. "Not seriously."

"Yes, seriously," she said. "But a three-dollar pair of earplugs saved our marriage." She patted his hand. "Now he just snores to kingdom come and I just sleep right through it."

They had slept through all the commotion. I was relieved. It saved me a lot of explanation, a lot of which I didn't have answers for myself.

CHAPTER NINETEEN

I waited in the newspaper office with my ad for the Pink Pineapple Tea and Thee. I used the same pineapple motif I'd stenciled on the sunroom floor and my menu covers, only smaller.

While I waited I glanced over the front page of *The Mess:* "Littleboro Women's Club Wins Tray," "4-H Helping Hands Win State Award," "Hoe and Hope Garden Club Announces Yard of the Month Winner." A whole town of real winners, I thought. I flipped pages. On the sports page I saw Homer Flooey had pulled in a twelve-pound bass. I wondered if that left any in the lake. I wondered if the water level went down when he pulled that big one out.

In the middle of the paper, near the fold and below an article and photograph of Barry Spender, who had made the Million Dollar Round Table in insurance, I read "Trial Set for Accused Killer." The housekeeper was listed; her name was Debbie Dellinger. Hmm, thought I, somehow the woman never looked to me like a Debbie. Debbie was sweet. Like Little Debbie Cookies or Debbie Reynolds with the smile and good cheer. Not someone in tight clothes and clear plastic heels who hotfooted it out of town with a whole truckload of furniture. The article said the trial would be held in Clinton and no date had been set. District Court got the big cases. I wondered if Ossie DelGardo would be pictured with the Accused in full glory. Ossie DelGardo with his jack-o'-lantern smile. His Bring 'Em Back Alive look like the man holding up his twelve-pound bass. Ossie had caught his killer and, better than that, he had hauled in a woman. That gave him extra points.

On page 2 was the photo of the new priest at St. Ann's. Black, I noticed. He was black. Good, I said to myself. He's what this town needs. He will shake up some set little social values and we will see who puts their religion over their racial prejudices. I wished him better luck than his predecessor. I felt a little cold wind at the back of my neck when I remembered finding Father Roderick. It seemed so long ago. Instead of only three weeks. So much had happened.

Out the window I saw a flash of pink and

lavender across the square. Crazy Reba flying her panties? I almost laughed out loud. When Reba bathed she also washed out her underwear in the bathwater. Or that's what Verna said. Then Reba took them back to her tree and hung them on the limbs to dry. Reba flies her flags, I thought. She's color in this place, this town where even this newspaper office is as dull and dusty and worn as Ethan Drummond's place. They had probably been furnished the same year, and since green plastic never died the chairs had never needed replacing.

Finally the secretary got off the phone and took my copy. She wrote up an order to run it every Wednesday for the next four issues. "Can you bill me?" I asked.

"Not if you don't have an account with us."

I wrote her a check and didn't look at the balance.

In the drugstore Malinda poked a pencil in her topknot as she came from behind the prescription counter. "Shopping for more bangles and spangles and beads?"

"Never again," I said.

"Did it work?"

"Haven't you seen Reba around town? You can almost feel the glow before she's in sight." I lifted both arms in the air. "At

Christmas the town can stand Reba on the courthouse lawn. She'll be a real living Christmas tree in all her sparkle and shine."

"Funny," Malinda said. "She never comes in here."

"I bet I know why," I said, and wrinkled my nose. "That old-fashioned medicine smell. I love it, but it reminds me of ear infections and chicken pox and sore throats and all the prescriptions I had from here as a child. I bet Reba remembers."

"I like the smell, too," Malinda said. "Every morning when I open up, it's still there and I take a deep breath. But then I never had sore throats or ear infections as a child."

"Nothing?" asked I.

"Remember I got the perfect attendance pin every year?"

"Among other things," I said. "And speaking of high school, do you remember Mr. Booth?"

"Mouse Ears Booth?" Malinda played with one of her gold hooped earrings. "How could I forget? I was the one who put the green snake down Freddie Folder's backpack at Lemon Lake. That garter snake is probably telling the tale to generations of garter snakes." She slapped her hip.

"Do you remember seeing something he

called wild parsley?"

"I remember poison ivy," Malinda said. "And pitcher plants . . . those long-necked bug-eating things."

"Somewhere near Lemon Lake grows wild parsley, and I'd like to find it."

"Won't the tame kind do? Any supermarket's got it."

"The tame kind isn't deadly poison."

"Got anybody in mind?" Malinda grinned.

"No, but somebody had Miss Lavinia marked for it."

"You don't trust the fine law-enforcement staff in this fine town?" Malinda asked. "You got to be the Little Red Hen and do it yourself?"

The truth was, I didn't trust anybody anymore except Malinda and Scott and Ida Plum . . . maybe. When Verna Crowell was mixed up in something, the rest of the town must be, too. Verna was your pillar of the community. She was your Sunday-school-teacher type. Your first-grade teacher. Your mama when your mama wasn't around. When the Verna Crowells of the community went bad, the rest of the world was heading downhill and racing like a bobsled.

"Make us a picnic supper." Malinda went to answer the phone. "And pick me up at home at six. I'll supply the wine and we'll go a'parsleying."

Before five, I had packed a pasta salad with peppers and almonds, cheeses and a loaf of pumpernickel still warm from the oven. Scott had taken the twin loaf after hinting in and out of the kitchen all afternoon about bread baking being his favorite perfume and how he thought flour on anyone's nose was a real turn-on. I ignored him.

"I don't know what your mama cooks," Ida Plum said, "but whatever it is, it doesn't fill you up." She was at the ironer again and I thought, Those two make a real team. Things get done.

"Who says I have a mother?" Scott asked, hammer poised over a nail. "I may have sprung fully formed from the loins of Apollo."

"Ha," Ida Plum said. "Double ha." I had told her about my wild night. The first thing she said was, "And you still haven't reported this? At least called Ossie."

I explained. She shook her head, hugged me. "I guess you know what you're doing." She stepped back to look at me. "Though sometimes I do wonder."

"Sure you don't want to take some muscle along?" Scott asked. "I know Malinda's going, and she can handle her own with a lot

227

of things."

"I'm pretty good at taking care of myself in certain situations, too," I said.

"You aren't going to at least call Ossie DelGardo?"

"No, I don't intend to. Not yet."

"Don't wait until it's too dangerous," Scott said at the door.

"I'm okay," I said. "I'm getting more okay every day. Trust me."

"I do trust you," Scott said. "I just don't trust the rest of the world out there." He pointed out the door.

"That's you!" Ida Plum called after him. "You are out there. Out of here!" She turned back to her work and I packed the rest of my picnic.

The house where Malinda had grown up was on a tree-lined, neat street next to Queentown. Rosalie kept the house so freshly painted it sparkled. It was a soft yellow, with white shutters. She had hanging baskets of ferns on the porch and planters tumbling tight with purple petunias. There was a vegetable garden out back, and in a month or so corn would be taller than the fence. And okra, squash, tomatoes, beets and green beans. I bet there were rows of zinnias and marigolds and hollyhocks beside the back wall.

I didn't have to go to the door. Malinda was waiting. She had changed to jeans and a Tar Heel T-shirt of Carolina blue. Malinda waved to the baby standing in the door. "God, he hates to see me go. Especially if I've just gotten home."

"I'm sorry," I said.

Malinda tucked wine in the basket. "No big deal. He's used to my undivided attention from the time I get home until he goes to bed. I read to him until he falls asleep. Want to hear me recite *Goodnight Moon*? All of Dr. Seuss? *Where the Wild Things Are*? *In the Night Kitchen*?"

"Spare me," I said. "But I'd like your thinking on where to go first. Somewhere in the back of my mind I keep thinking behind the dam . . . that area."

"First we eat," Malinda said. "I'll think while I chew."

At the park we ate sitting on the end of the pier. The lake was empty. The paddle-boats were still docked and shelved from winter. The concession stand wouldn't open until after Memorial Day. That was the official start of summer and Labor Day the end. Someone grilled hot dogs on the hill near the shelter. From the tennis courts we heard a steady *whump, whump, thack.*

Malinda layered cheese, ham and lettuce

229

on pumpernickel spread with hot herb mustard. "Wonderful," she said. "I'm thinking already."

I told her about last night.

"I would have aimed lower," Malinda said. "That's where it really gets them." Then she laughed. "Of course, he wouldn't be as easily spotted around town then, would he? Just walking sideways . . . if he was walking at all."

"All I remember of Booth's field trips seems to be swampy places or places between bogs and marshes.

"That sounds like behind the dam."

We locked the picnic things in the car. I tied my blouse in a knot at my waist, pulled on a cotton hat, then picked up my plastic bag, botany book and scissors.

We walked around the end of the dam. Someone had dumped a rotten rowboat in the willows along with several old tires, rusted buckets and junk in general. "The Hoe and Hope folks ought to come inspect this scenic little corner of Littleboro," I said. "Watch for snakes."

"Snakes watch for me," Malinda said. "I make enough noise to tell them I'm coming." She brushed back shrubs and low limbs as we climbed the hill.

The sun was orange neon, a copper ball

coloring everything in a strange, strong light.

"This is the backside of nowhere," I said.

"Those were Booth's favorite places."

We crossed a swamp below the hill, then through more woods. "I used to listen to my mama and stay away from woods like this," Malinda said. "Too bad she never warned me about the wide-open places as well."

I didn't press. I suspected both of us could hang regrets like rags from every bush we passed.

Malinda walked a fallen log across a ravine. "Ha, I'm not in such bad shape after all."

I followed through brambles and briars.

"Oops," Malinda said, stopping. "Here's where we detour. There's enough poison ivy to itch all of Littleboro the rest of the summer and half into winter."

We crawled over a wire fence topped with twisted barbs, holding down the cutting edge for each other.

"Anything familiar to you yet?" I asked.

"My first trilliums this year." Malinda sighed. "Look. But we're not looking for beauty . . . we're hunting evil. Wonder if anyone ever died from eating a trillium?"

"Just wild parsley," I said. "And I think I see something in that low place that looks green and frilly. Something a garden club lady would like." I had told Malinda Booth's story about the garden club ladies luncheon and the parsley look alike. . . . and Malinda whooped. She didn't remember it. "That's probably when I was catching that poor garter snake that probably hasn't recovered yet."

I examined the plant. "Remember how to key?" I asked. "Your flora formula?"

" '*Conium maculatum,* botanical name. Common name: poison hemlock, lesser hemlock, deadly hemlock, poison parsley, muskrat weed. Deadly parts: all; the poisonous leaves can be made into a fatal salad,' " Malinda read. "I think you found what did in Miss Lavinia. But who put the parsley on her plate? It didn't get there by itself."

I snipped off several specimens and carefully slid them into my plastic sandwich bag.

The sky had become a thick gray and was darkening fast. "Do we go back the way we came or is it closer to walk out to the road, walk back to the car that way?" I asked.

"If they haven't moved the road, it's closer," Malinda said, and started down the hill ahead of me.

Suddenly there was a yelp and Malinda slid down a muddy slope and disappeared.

"Malinda?" I called. There was a muffled,

watery kind of answer that sounded desperate. "Malinda?"

"Here!" Malinda called. "Here! Help me!"

Malinda had landed in a black bog and foundered, slipping, splashing back as she tried to reach for an overhanging limb, a low-growing bush . . . anything she could grab to keep from sliding under again.

I searched for a limb on the ground that I could hold out to Malinda. Nothing. There was nothing. I thought of taking off my shirt, but that wouldn't reach. But I had something that would. Quickly I stripped off my jeans and, holding the end of one leg, knotted the other and threw it to Malinda, who slid, reached for it and missed.

I threw the jeans again. This time they landed closer, floated in the thick foam, bobbed. Malinda grabbed the knot. She held on, coughing, as I braced my foot against a boulder and pulled. I pulled until my arms felt stretched from my body, stretched until they were no longer a part of me.

Malinda crawled onto the bank. She sprawled on the ground, coughing and gagging. I helped her to a dry place in the pines, Malinda dripping, covered with slimy tags that hung from her like bright green fringe. She reeked of decay and stagnated water.

"I owe," Malinda coughed, choking, coughed again.

"You owe me nothing." I hugged her. "It's my fault we're here in the first place."

"Yeah." Malinda stood and shook herself, squeezed water from her hair. "If I'd gone down again, you'd never live with the guilt. I know you. See what a bundle of bad vibes I saved you?"

"I owe you," I said. "We're even. Leave it that way."

"Let's go home," Malinda said. "That was no natural wonder that tried to suck me under."

"What do you mean?"

"That sucker was man-made." Malinda took off her blouse and twisted water from it. "I mean dug. Somebody dug a pit . . . a cotton-picking moat. The sides of that thing were smooth and you dropped into it too suddenly. Nature's too kind for that. She warns you."

"So, whose property is this? People don't go around digging eight-foot ditches in public parks."

"I think we passed the park when we climbed that wire fence," Malinda said. She rested again on the pine needles and tried to dry her hair, which hung in her eyes and was pasted to her neck and shoulders.

"If that way is the cemetery," I said, and pointed east in the darkening sky, "then this way goes toward Miss Tempie's."

"It's her land, then," Malinda said.

"And her trap, and her parsley . . ."

". . . that killed Miss Lavinia."

There was a sound of twigs being broken. The crisp, quick snap, then silence.

Malinda and I looked at each other.

Malinda whispered, "I've got a feeling somebody heard every word we said."

CHAPTER TWENTY

There was an envelope in my door the next morning. When I removed the note, a dried, dead old bug fell out and I read in spidery handwriting: "Come to tea honoring me. Five this afternoon. Tempie Merritt." I laughed. I wouldn't go for the world. The nerve of that woman. Not even an "I would like you to" or a "Please," but "Come to tea." Not on your life. I crumpled the yellowed paper, threw it in the trash, then scooped the bug back into the envelope and dumped it in as well.

Whoever left the note prowled the streets early in the morning or late at night or both. Crazy Reba wasn't the only nocturnal creeper around.

There had been no guests at the Dixie Dew last night. For one thing, I hadn't been home to receive them if any came. I told Ida Plum, when we cleaned up after the Harltons left, that as slow as things were . . .

after their bang-up start, I'd call her when I and the Dixie Dew needed her.

"Humph," Ida Plum said. "That may be too late the way you been living your life lately." But Ida Plum had made sure all the beds were freshly made, the linen closet stacked and looking like an ad in *Organize Your Home* magazine, before she took her sweater off the hanger in the pantry, draped it around her shoulders and started out. "You be careful," she said. Ida Plum stood in the doorway and I half expected her to point her finger and lecture, but she didn't. Her tone of voice had done that. "You don't know the ways of Littleboro anymore. Things change underneath more than they change where you can see them and it's not always for the better." She wheeled on her heel and was halfway down the walk before I could ask, "What things? What do you know?"

If Ida Plum knew so much and continually warned me to be careful, why couldn't she tell me what she knew about what was going on? Sometimes I wondered if Ida Plum might only be working here to keep an eye on me for Miss Tempie. Or Verna. Or whoever else had my immediate demise in mind. Ida Plum certainly wasn't working for the pay. Not with what I'd been paying her. Maybe somebody else was paying her. But why?

After last night, I wouldn't be surprised at anything anybody would do. Man-made slime pits. I shuddered to think what would have happened if either me or Malinda had gone that way alone.

Last night after I dropped Malinda off . . . Malinda who rode home wrapped in our picnic tablecloth saying she'd have to take ten showers to get the stench out and she was headed there straight as her squeaky sneakers would take her . . . I took a long bath myself. I soaked and read and thought. I'd nearly drowned Malinda in my wild parsley chase and had endangered both our lives. All for what? To find the root of what was going on in this town. Nobody else seemed interested. Ossie DelGardo might consider murder too much to be a part of his job, but when it happened in my house and almost happened again . . . to me, then somebody had to do something.

Tea with Miss Tempie? Of course I wasn't going. I had better things to do. I'd rather scrape ghastly gray paint off the double doors that opened to the dining room. I'd rather paint moldings. I'd rather do any-thing.

At ten Scott arrived towing two electricians he introduced as Bob and Bill, the Mitchell brothers. "Bob plays bass and Bill plays fiddle."

Scott must have read my look, because he quickly added, "When they're not stringing hot and cold wire."

The brothers — one had a red beard; the other was bald — wore matching dull blue uniforms with *ACE* embroidered on the backs.

"They're bona fide," Scott added. "In fact" — he laid an arm across Bill's shoulder — "they're the best."

The three went to the attic. Later I heard them in the basement, yelling things back and forth.

Just before lunch, Malinda telephoned. "You going to go play tea party?"

"Not this girl," I said, wondering why Malinda got an invitation, too.

"I'm game if you are. Always wanted to put on my hat and gloves, go to the front door of that house. Hell, I always wanted to be invited to that house."

"Miss Tempie's?"

"Honey," Malinda said, "that house was the awe of my childhood. My grandmother cooked for them. Once in a while I got to hang around the kitchen and peek through a crack in the door at the goings-on, but that was as far as I got."

"What went on?" I scraped paint as I listened.

"Not that one," Malinda said in the background. "There." I could almost see her pointing out an aisle to someone in the drugstore, then turning her attention back to me. "Nothing. That's just it. That house was so filled with anger and silence, it sulked. Her daddy tippled in a big way, and the mother was just this side of the crazy farm."

"I didn't know," I said.

"You ever thought how sudden this tea party is? I mean, what brought this on?"

"You don't believe in bolts from the blue?"

"I believe I know who heard us splashing around in the ooze last night."

"And here we go back for more?"

"Why not? I'm going for my mama, my grandmama and me. It's time." Malinda's voice said she had made up her mind.

"See you at the front gate at five," I said, wondering what I'd gotten myself into.

Back at the Dixie Dew Scott took my scraper and worked on the door. "Don't eat anything fishy," he said.

"You know?" I asked Scott. "About this lovely invitation to what promises to be a lovely tea with Miss Tempie?"

He must have overheard me on the phone to Ida Plum who said, "You and Malinda are asking for trouble. This whole idea sounds suspicious to me. I think you ought to mind your own business, such as it is, and stay home." She slammed down the phone. I knew in my heart of hearts she was right, but this "invite" seemed a way to get to the bottom of all this nasty stuff.

"I heard, and I can guess. Stay way away from the Nine Lives Paté," he said, paint flakes falling in a shower around him.

I leaned around the dining room door and poked my tongue at him. "I'll put it in my napkin and bring it home to you."

Sherman rubbed her ankle. "No, not you." I laughed.

Guests checked in at two. A retired teacher who had lavender hair. Ms. Joyce Linski. She looked like a stick wearing big glasses. The man with her was round and red and slightly damp all over. He wore an embroidered shirt. Had puffy little hands. "Norman Small." He took my hand in both of his and patted it warmly.

"My friend," Ms. Linski said. "He will take the rear bedroom and a nap."

They started up the stairs as one of the electrician brothers came down. Bill or Bob took their bags and said, "Don't mind us, ma'am; we're mostly overhead."

"Low sodium!" Ms. Linski called back. "Only fruit for him for breakfast. But I'll take eggs and a muffin . . . if it's homemade. And diet butter!"

She sounded so immediate, I started to remind her breakfast was usually in the morning, and a good eighteen hours away, but Ms. Linski said, "We've brought our own dinner, and we have work to do."

"Work?" I asked.

"Conferences don't just happen. They have to be planned and somebody has to do it."

"I see," I said. Murders don't just happen, I thought. They have to be planned, and somebody has to do it. But me? Who planned and murdered Miss Lavinia Lovingood and Father Roderick? Tried to murder me? May have murdered Mama Alice? One busy little person or several working together?

"Yoo-hoo." Verna Crowell came from the kitchen. "I came over to see if you wanted some lovely little zucchini squash. They were at the Farmer's Market and I couldn't resist them."

I knew Verna didn't buy the zucchini because she couldn't resist them. They were meant to be a peace offering, and I could

242

sniff, say I never touched the things, or be gracious, rise above the situation and act out Mama Alice's proverb "pretty is as pretty does."

"Thank you, Verna," I said, and took the green-striped things. "That was thoughtful."

"You probably do the little boat things with them, but I don't go to all the trouble. They're sweet fried in with broccoli and peppers. Try that."

"I'll make zucchini bread," I said. "This is still a bed-and-breakfast . . . not a tearoom yet."

Verna giggled. She actually put her bony fingers over her face and giggled. "Tempie's the one having tea."

I stopped putting the zucchini in the refrigerator and turned to Verna. "You're going, too?"

"Wouldn't miss it," Verna said. "When Tempie calls, you come running or you are through in this town. That's what Father Roderick found out."

"What?" I asked. "What about Father Roderick?"

Verna started out the door and I wanted to grab her shoulders and stop her, but Verna turned. "Let Tempie tell you. She knows it all," she said in a snappish voice, then set her lips in a hard line.

I knew I'd get nothing else. What Verna knew she wouldn't tell. And maybe Miss Tempie did want to talk. After all, she was honoring herself. Tacky, Mama Alice would have hooted. "Tacky" was giving yourself a bridal shower. "Tacky" was sending printed thank-you notes for gifts instead of hand-written monogrammed ones. So Miss Tempie was being about as tacky as tacky could get. But if she had some answers for me, she could be as tacky as she wanted.

CHAPTER TWENTY-ONE

I stood in front of wrought-iron gates with a huge *M* in the middle. The Merritts never did anything small, and the iron in that gate looked thick enough to keep out anybody, friend or enemy.

The hot afternoon sun felt like a heavy hand on the top of my head, even through my white lace "picture" hat. I found the hat nestled in tissue paper in a gold and black hatbox in the attic. Mama Alice always said if you keep something and wait twenty-five years it will come back in style. I didn't know which style was in at the moment and I didn't care much past blue jeans, but something told me I needed to show up at Miss Tempie's in a hat that said I could give as well as I got.

I didn't even have to dust the hat; I just shook it a little, put it on and walked out the door.

I didn't see Verna on the way over and I

didn't care. Verna was so nutty, she'd take a light after-lunch nap and sleep through the afternoon, wake just in time for the sherry hours. If I was lucky, that's what Verna had done today. If I wasn't, Verna would be there, chattering away about something that didn't matter. Verna would say anything to keep from saying what you really wanted to know, what you needed and wanted to hear.

I stared at the tall white house that loomed like a castle at the end of the magnolia-lined driveway. The Merritts had picked the highest hill in town to build on, a town they'd owned most of at one time. Probably they still owned some of the empty buildings downtown that couldn't be rented, should anybody have a burning desire to start a booming business in a dying, decayed little town. Most of the buildings had leaky roofs, broken windows and weak floors. And low property tax bills. Probably pocket change for people like the Merritts.

Frankly, I thought, the Merritt house didn't look much better than half the empty buildings downtown. Windows on the third floor were missing shutters or were broken and boarded up. I admired the beautiful blue balls in the lightning rods on the roof, but even some of the rods were broken, bent and twisted.

A wooden balcony jutted from a second-floor window. It hung loose with one side askew. Sad, I thought, a house this elegant falling apart.

To the rear of the house, I saw a structure that had once been a greenhouse. Now only a few panes of glass glinted and weeds tall as trees shot up through the rest.

Inside this mess, I thought, lives Miss Tempie Merritt, who never lets you forget she was a Juilliard scholar and once played a concert tour. She loved to lavish all that information around. The old frump. And she dressed in clothes so old they were almost back in style again. Thin cottons with square lace collars, tucks, dropped waistlines; Miss Tempie even let her slip show before teens wore slips as dresses. She loved to point out her hand-tatted lace edging.

The old bird, I thought as I rubbed one of the gate's iron finials that was old and heavy in my hand. Miss Tempie could hold one hell of a yard sale. Probably every piece of furniture ever bought for the house was still there. She'd hang on to everything until her last breath, then try to take it with her if she could. Tempie had probably left it all to her poodle, but Harold had done some lawyer a big favor and died first. Now Miss Tempie was probably stewing up a new will and driving Ethan Drummond crazy.

I sighed. A little breeze ran through new maple leaves in the thick forest on each side of the gate. I pictured Miss Tempie sitting up nights clipping newspaper coupons for cat food.

A Jeep wagon slowed. Malinda honked and waved. "I'm parking here," she said. "That driveway looks tough on tires." She hopped out, slammed the door.

"Where's your hat?" I asked.

"You kidding? I may do a lot of things, but wearing hats isn't one of them."

"Gloves either?" I inspected Malinda's hands. "I thought you said this was a hat and glove occasion."

"Mental gloves." Malinda held both hands out, wiggled her fingers. "I'm careful what I touch and even more careful what I eat." She opened the gate. Huge hinges gave rusty, deep-throated groans.

I connected the sound with being trapped in the mausoleum, and it wasn't a fond memory.

"If it smells fishy . . ." Malinda pushed the gate open and left it. "In case we have to leave on the run . . . If it smells fishy . . . I'm passing it up."

"Just because I've been behind her in line at the grocery checkout and know she doesn't own a cat isn't proof positive."

"It's proof enough for me." Malinda locked her car and dropped the keys in her pocket. "That driveway looks rough on panty hose, too. Lucky I'm not wearing any."

Grasshoppers leaped and whirred in the weeds and gravel, then sat and buzzed like rattlesnakes.

"This place is snaky," I said, eyeing the waist-high weeds.

"All snakes don't live in the grass," Malinda said. "Some dig pits and fill them with goo for little girls to fall into."

"No pits here," I said, picking my way. "Just pitchforks we may be walking into." I'd worn a blue shirtwaist dress but wished now I'd worn jeans. The dress made me feel vulnerable and less able to move swiftly if I had to.

Malinda wore a denim shirt that kept getting hooked by briars.

A flock of crows chased a blue jay that screamed overhead. The crows' cawing sounded like laughter, cruel and teasing.

My heels sank in the gravel between briars. Several times briars whipped and scratched my legs.

"Long drives may be impressive," Malinda said. "But who cares? I'm so hungry I'll eat the icing off the pan."

"What?" I said. "You mean bowl."

"No," Malinda said, "I mean I'll eat icing off the pan. It's an old family story. Remind me to tell you sometime when we aren't picking our way through briars."

The driveway widened and the weeds and briars thinned. My legs still burned from the scratches that felt raw and bleeding.

"A couple of coats of paint wouldn't hurt this place," Malinda said. "My mama would have painted or moved out a long time ago."

Behind huge white columns stood a wide concrete porch piled with dead leaves and fallen branches. Shrubbery grew almost as high as the second-story windows.

"Bet that roof leaks," I said. "I bet it's leaked for years."

We stood before huge double doors that had tall leaded fanlights in an arch above them. I twisted the doorbell that felt corroded. The bell gave an ugly rasp that echoed inside as if the house might be empty.

"What if the whole thing is a hoax," Malinda asked, "and there's nobody here? I can't believe anyone lives like this." She glanced at the debris on the porch, the cracked windows and bare wood showing where paint had cracked off completely.

To the rear of the house both of us noticed

a freshly mowed area of grass, not weeds, and a planter perky with pansies. There was some new order in all this chaos. Some attempt.

We started to go around back, toward the mowed area, when one of the front doors opened.

Verna Crowell stood holding Robert Redford. She wore a faded green cotton housecoat and pearls.

Malinda poked me in the ribs.

"They're in the solarium," Verna said. She had her eyes made up, and a round red spot of rouge like cartoon characters wore sat high on each cheek. They? I wondered who, besides Miss Tempie, was in the solarium.

"Kinky," Malinda whispered behind me. "This is kinky."

Verna stiffened, drew herself up and held the rabbit closer. "He's a rabbit, not a cat." She glared at Melinda. "His name is Robert Redford." She turned and we followed her from the foyer with its glass chandelier so dust hung and cobweb woven it would take six men scrubbing and two tubs of water to ever get it to shine, through smeared glass doors into a huge, dark hall that loomed with furniture and heavy oil portraits and was packed high with boxes.

"Lord," Malinda muttered under her

breath, "is this where dirt goes to die?"

"Oops." I bumped a box tall enough to contain a coffin stored on end. Whatever was in the box didn't shift half an inch, and my thigh ached as if I'd hit a boulder.

The hall smelled of mildew, rotten fabric, old furniture and filth. We passed several sets of double doors locked with bolts as big as arms.

Verna put Robert Redford down and the rabbit hopped like he knew where to go. Verna hummed a little tune I tried to recognize until I gave up. Either the tune wasn't to a song I knew or Verna was making it up as she went along. The rabbit stopped once and scratched under his red halter. Verna waited for him. I saw glass doors ahead and light.

When Verna opened the doors, sunlight stung my eyes.

"It is an abrupt change, isn't it?" Verna asked.

The solarium was so thick with plants, my first thought was, A jungle. We'll need machetes to hack our way through. But Verna went smoothly around a tree and led us down a path. There had once been an indoor pool in the solarium, but over the years someone had filled it with soil, compost, whatever, and Miss Tempie had a regular vegetable garden growing there with cornstalks five feet high, tomato plants, okra and peas. Cucumber and squash plants tumbled from wooden tubs along the walls.

At a patio table spread with an irregular cloth, Miss Tempie sat wearing a straw hat. She'd tied a scarf over it that she knotted under her chin. On her arms she wore blue lace mitts, probably left from some prom or wedding fifty years ago. They covered liver spots and saggy old arms. There's no pride like old Southern pride, I thought.

"Girls," Miss Tempie said. "Girls, do come sit down."

There were five chairs at the table. I saw Malinda count, too. There's four of us including Miss Tempie, I added in my head, and no one else was in the room. Was this a séance? And the empty chair for a ghost? Would Miss Lavinia reappear in her night-gown? Or her beautiful eel-skin suit, the one she was buried in?

The cornstalks parted and there stood a man holding a shovel. His right hand wore a thick bandage. "Oh," I remembered, and my head began to ache. I couldn't see his face, but I knew his size and shape. Rolfe, the man who had been with Miss Tempie in the cemetery. Her handyman, chauffeur, gardener . . . whatever dirty thing she needed doing.

Malinda saw the man and the hand at the same time. She nodded at me. "This isn't to be an all-female party after all," she murmured.

Robert Redford suddenly bumped Miss Tempie's chair and bounded under the table, rocking it. Dishes clattered and Miss Tempie continued to pour a hot steady stream of tea that missed the cup completely and ran in a little brown stream on the tablecloth.

The rabbit shot out the other side of the table and Verna darted after him.

The soft scraping sound of a shovel being sent into the soil and lifted out again made my spine tingle. The man was shoveling a hole.

"Don't mind Rolfe." Miss Tempie paused in her pouring. She held the pot aloft and gestured with her other arm. "I simply feel one must return to the soil what one can, when one can."

Rolfe was burying something, I realized. But what? Rows of corn nearly hid him. All I could see was a torn black T-shirt that read "Jesus Saves" in large silver letters across the back.

"We owe a duty to the earth," Miss Tempie said. "A debt that must be paid." She looked with milky old eyes toward the ceiling.

Paid with murder? I wanted to ask, but didn't. Instead, I picked up my napkin . . . it was pink and faded where it had been folded. There was a rust spot the color of dried blood in one corner.

I noticed Malinda unfolded her napkin also. Aren't we the prim and proper ones? I thought. Present at what could be our last meal if we weren't careful, and we came of our own accord. Curiosity killed the cat. It could kill us.

Miss Tempie emptied the rest of the tea and said, "I can't believe we've run out already." She got up and tottered toward the kitchen.

"Dishwater's stronger than that stuff," Malinda said. "It's so thin I could read a newspaper through it."

I choked a nervous giggle, then coughed. There was a dry spot in my throat that tickled. I kept coughing, the man kept digging and Malinda glanced around, pointed to the missing glass overhead, the smudged and dirty windows that were either cracked or half-broken.

Birds flew in, came and went through the missing windows. They winged and squeaked as they dipped down into the garden.

"Why are we doing this?" Malinda shivered. "I've been in slums I felt safer in."

"Because somebody killed Miss Lavinia Lovingood and Father Roderick . . . but not necessarily both. We've got to find out."

Verna came back, balancing a huge silver tray so heavy she rocked and swayed carrying it. She thunked it on the table. "Girls, when you get my age, don't go around thinking you can do anything you used to."

On the tray were rows of vanilla wafers and thin lemon cookies arranged on a stained and crumpled paper doily.

"Can you get salmonella from cookies?" I mumbled to Malinda.

"Only if they're filled with warm chicken salad," she said.

Miss Tempie tottered in, sandwich tray in one hand, teapot in the other.

"And speaking of chicken salad . . ." Malinda whispered.

"I make my own," Miss Tempie said. "I always have." She held the tray toward me and I hesitated. The sandwiches were nestled in parsley and decorated on top with parsley. They probably had parsley in the filling. Or what most people thought was parsley until it was too late. What Miss Lavinia mistook for parsley?

"I'm allergic," I said.

"Now, I've never heard that," Miss Tempie said. "Allergic to what? Certainly not chicken. Not my chicken salad with home-made mayonnaise and a little kiss of curry . . ." She puckered her mouth. "Oh, it is the best stuff." She put a sandwich on my plate, then two on Malinda's, her old bony fingers blue and swift. "You must take at least a bite. That's only good manners."

I ate a cookie that was dry, crumbly, and tasted like mothballs.

Verna took a sandwich, broke it in half and nibbled like a rabbit.

"Don't." I reached out my hand to stop Verna mid-sandwich.

"Honey," she said, holding her sandwich out of my reach. "I helped Tempie make these and this is my lunch. I walked over here." She finished the sandwich and took another.

Miss Tempie ate sandwiches, too, her tongue clicking slightly as she chewed. "I think there's nothing better. And better for you. People today don't eat right. That's what's wrong with half the world."

Malinda dipped a cookie in her tea, shrugged and gave me a half smile that said she could dunk and sip with the best of them. She even held out her little finger as she dunked.

The shoveling stopped and there were muffled sounds, then the shovel again. Another hole being dug? There were two of us and two graves waiting where no one would ever think to look. Certainly not members of our fine local law enforcement. If they ever thought to come looking here, Miss Tempie would give them cookies and tea and they'd bow and scrape to old Southern customs, the mystique of sweet Southern little old ladies.

Finally, Rolfe packed the earth around the holes, stamping with what sounded like huge feet. I remembered the sound of those feet. How they thumped and bumped down the hall to my bedroom. What did he plan to bury? I'm not sure I wanted to know.

"Too bad Father Roderick couldn't be here," Miss Tempie said. "He liked my chicken salad so much. He even asked me especially to make it for Lavinia that day we had tea."

"What day?" I asked.

"The day she came back. Came back to Littleboro to live."

"Ha," Verna said. "Ha on you. She didn't come back to Littleboro to live. She came back to die."

"But she didn't plan it that way." Miss Tempie sniffed.

"None of us do." Verna looked at her hands holding another sandwich. "We never do." Her voice quivered a little. "And you said it would be like old times. Lavinia, you and me, having our little parties, going shopping, doing things together. That's what I wanted."

"That's not what Lavinia wanted," Miss Tempie said. Her eyes were black as two burnt coals now. I felt I could feel the heat from them. "She wanted it all and she would have gotten it like she did the first time."

"You got the house," Verna said.

They seemed to have forgotten Malinda and I were in the room.

"But that's all. Not enough to keep it up. Not even enough each month to buy myself a new hat." She patted her hair. "At least once a season, I went to New York to buy hats. I was known for my hats." Miss Tempie's face clouded, darkened and looked hard. Then it softened suddenly as if she remembered she had been speaking and there were other people in the room. She tried to smile, and to keep her voice level, but there was an undercrust of thick ice, hate huge as an iceberg that could sink a battleship. "Until Lavinia's father took everything away."

259

"Took it?" Verna asked suddenly. "Took it? My foot! From what I heard, your daddy lost everything he had to Tevis Lovingood and didn't leave you so much as a pot to pee in. Haw." Verna started laughing. "Haw." She slapped the table at her own joke and Robert Redford jumped down and ran into the garden. He sat at the edge of a row of beets and cleaned himself like a cat.

Miss Tempie chose to ignore Verna, lifted her shoulders and went on. "My father was an excellent businessman. He owned half of this county. And horse farms. He had seven. We even went to the Kentucky Derby once. He was a state senator twice . . . but that was before Tevis Lovingood had to have his turn."

"Not what I heard," Verna said. She shrugged, looked at us and winked. "Of course this was all before my time."

"Was not." Miss Tempie glared at her, widened her nostrils. "You're a year older than me and you know it."

"Younger," Verna said. "Two years younger."

The two women stared at each other like two cats with their backs raised.

"Lavinia was in the middle," Verna said. "Till you killed her." She reached for another sandwich.

"Stop." Miss Tempie hit Verna's hand. "You'll make yourself sick."

Verna held the sandwich tight and twisted out of Miss Tempie's reach. "Well, you know you did. I said, 'Tempie, you shouldn't. You shouldn't.'" She turned to me and Malinda. "But did she listen to me? No." Verna beat the table with her index finger. "No, she did not."

I turned to Malinda and our expressions asked each other, Can we be hearing this? This is not your normal tea party conversation.

"I had to," Miss Tempie said. "Besides, it wasn't like really killing her. At her age it was only a matter of months, a few years anyway, and this way she got it over with. I did her a favor. Lavinia was always so vain."

Tape recorder, I thought suddenly. I wish I had a tape recorder. Will anybody believe this? Ossie DelGardo? Not in a million years. And somehow I couldn't see Miss Tempie on trial for murder. In jail? Not Miss Tempie. Not Verna either. I glanced at Malinda, who drank tea. At least I've got a witness, eye- and ear witness, but doesn't that make us accessories? Knowing something like this? I almost giggled. Accessories always made me think of scarves and hand-bags, jewelry. Was the tea getting to me?

What was in it? I'd worried about sandwiches, forgotten about tea. Now I could be really poisoned! I felt a little nauseated already.

"Father Roderick was a different story," Miss Tempie said, sipping her tea. "I had nothing to do with him." She set her teacup down and spread both hands in the air. "With the little strength I've got left in these hands, I can't even open a jar of jelly, much less twist some piece of silk around somebody's neck." She touched her throat, made a face. "Awful way to die."

"Any way is awful," I said, thinking the tea must be okay after all. We were all drinking it.

"Not Lavinia." Miss Tempie played with the diamonds on her fingers. "Weak heart. I knew she'd eat the parsley. She's always been so picky, picky."

"Didn't she taste that it wasn't parsley?" I asked. The question popped from my mouth before I could stop it.

Miss Tempie looked at me impatiently. She paused before she answered. "Of course I expect it was a little bit bitter, but I knew Lavinia would be too polite to say anything."

Polite to the end! I thought. This woman has been a little bit crazy for years and everybody only thought, Eccentric, that's just the way Miss Tempie is. Now she's killed somebody. And she's sitting here calmly talking about it like she's discussing a Sunday school lesson.

But Ossie DelGardo had found traces of hemlock in Miss Lavinia's body.

"Honey, I worried I'd never get her to eat enough parsley. Parsley," she said, and laughed. "I was doing her a favor, only she didn't know it. Such a clean and neat way to die. I knew Lavinia always dressed so for bed. Particular. She dressed like she was going someplace special . . . all that lace." Miss Tempie sighed.

"I sleep in flannel myself," Verna said. "Year-round." She smiled wide, her teeth yellow as old ivory.

"I don't believe this," I muttered. I pushed away the parsley on my plate. Or was it wild hemlock? I wanted to sneak some of it into my purse in case someone needed to identify it later. I could see how *The Mess* would word it now. "And the evidence of the death was found upon the deceased's person." How much did it take to do in somebody? Miss Tempie had used the wild parsley and somehow gotten Miss Lavinia to eat enough of it to do her in. "Why?" I asked.

"It's such a long story." Miss Tempie sighed and looked around the room.

Was she looking for Rolfe? Had he gone or was he still standing in the corn rows? I couldn't see. The sky was darkening, the room getting a dusky blue-gray and there were no lights. None I could see. Not overhead, nor on the walls.

"Boring, boring," said Verna, whose eyes were bright as wine.

"It always makes me cry to talk about it." Miss Tempie sniffed.

I poked Malinda. She'd not said anything in so long. Was she doing more than listening to these two? "Let's go," I whispered, low enough surely neither Miss Tempie nor Verna heard.

"Oh, it was some show all right," Miss Tempie said.

Malinda nudged me, pointed to the glass door behind us, then touched her watch, held up five fingers, whispered, "Five minutes."

Both of us saw a shadow move outside the door. Rolfe. He carried the shovel like a weapon.

Would we get out of this place alive? And if we didn't, would Miss Tempie get away with killing us like she had Miss Lavinia? If she had indeed killed Miss Lavinia? At this point, with these two crazies, I didn't know who or what to believe.

I tried to remember if anyone knew we were here and would come looking. But would they come looking too late? Scott knew, but would he take these two women seriously? He had joked about the tea party. But this was no joke.

The shadow stopped, stood at the door and waited.

CHAPTER TWENTY-TWO

Whoever it was — Rolfe, I thought, from the bulk of the shadow — had stood by the door briefly, then left.

Malinda sighed audibly. "At the count of five," she said, "starting now."

"Margaret Alice never knew." Verna drank tea.

"One," said Malinda.

"Wait." I put an arm out to stop Malinda, who dodged past it and sprinted for the door, where she rattled the knob frantically.

"Locked," I said.

"Stuck," said Miss Tempie, fiddling with another sandwich. "You girls. I'm surprised at both of you. No manners. You don't ever leave until you've told your hostess you had a nice time. I don't know about young people these days. They're so narcissistic."

"Not like us, our generation," Verna said. "Why, you take Margaret Alice. She'd give you anything she had."

"And you killed her," I blurted to Verna. "You pushed her."

Verna pushed out her lower lip and looked hurt. "Oh, Bethie honey, I'd never do a thing like that. I told you Margaret Alice was my best friend."

"Not mine," Miss Tempie said.

Malinda took her chair again, her face flushed, eyes slightly wider and frightened. Or angry? Some of both, I decided.

"Margaret Alice wouldn't sell that house to the church," Miss Tempie said.

"I never knew they wanted it," I said.

"They still do, honey," Verna said. "And they'll get it."

"Why? What does that little church want with Mama Alice's house?" I hugged myself for strength and protection. "My house." Things shifted in place in my mind . . . the break-in, intruder, trapping me in a mausoleum . . . all of it.

"The church," Verna whispered. "Big business. Big bucks."

Miss Tempie wasn't involved in big business. Not that bat brain. No way. "If you didn't push Mama Alice" — I had to get an answer and now was my chance — "who the hell did?" I stood over Verna and grabbed her shoulder.

Verna choked on her tea, sputtered and

sprayed the tablecloth, my arm. "Nobody," she said. "Nobody."

I shook Verna's arm. I'd get the truth out if I had to shake it out. I caught Malinda's eyes and read, I'm with you. We can take them.

Verna collapsed back in her chair. "I found her."

"Just like you said when you called me?" I let Verna go.

"It was a stroke."

"All that time in the hospital and nursing home," Miss Tempie said. "And those things cost you an arm and a leg." She giggled. "I thought we'd get a lien."

"And you almost did," I said bitterly. "The nursing home took everything she had . . . but the house. That was next."

"I got lost somewhere in all this. Who took what from whom? As my mama would make me say," Malinda asked in a voice that sounded like she meant business.

"I thought Verna killed Mama Alice," I said. "I found a note that said Mama Alice was pushed, and it was Verna's handwriting."

"Tempie made me do it." Verna sat straighter in her chair. "It was her idea."

"Well, now we know she wasn't, so what harm did it do?" Miss Tempie seemed impatient. "Honestly, such a fuss over four words."

"It isn't the words," I said. "It's the deeds. And you've done some dirty ones."

"All in the name of the Lord," Miss Tempie said. "It's His house . . . for His glory."

"Foot," Verna said. "To cover your tail. That's all."

"Whoa," I said. "Back up. I want some answers and I want them here and now and I'm not leaving until I get them."

"As if we could," Malinda mumbled.

"It's this way," Verna said, then stopped. She put her hand to her forehead and slumped to the table, her face falling in her plate.

No one moved for a moment. Then Miss Tempie made a sound of disgust with her lips. "She gets overwrought. Then one little sip of sherry and she's out." There must have been sherry in Verna's tea. Miss Tempie's, too? I hadn't tasted any in mine.

Someone moved behind the double glass doors and Miss Tempie tapped her saucer with a spoon.

Rolfe came to her elbow.

"Verna has left us," Miss Tempie said. "Momentarily." She indicated for Rolfe to remove her. "Let her nap in my bedroom."

She dismissed both of them with a little wave of her hand.

Rolfe slid his large hands under Verna's arms and lifted her carefully from her chair as if she weighed nothing at all.

His right hand was wrapped in a bandage thick as a blanket. I heard Malinda draw in her breath at the sight of the telltale hand. "Easy," she said. "Easy."

Rolfe carried Verna from the room.

Miss Tempie rearranged her tea things with a great clinking and clattering of cups, saucers and spoons. "It's really such a simple little story and it's a shame you girls have been so curious to hear it. I fear you'll have to stay here, once you know."

"Why?" I asked. "Why did you invite us to come?"

"Why, honey," Miss Tempie said, "I have to kill you. Absolutely *have* to. Sweet girls, both of you, but you can't go poking around in other people's business."

"But," I said, and looked at Malinda, who rolled her eyes.

Miss Tempie kept on, a crazy wide smile across her wrinkle-creviced face. "If you girls hadn't found the hemlock down by my own private little pond. Ha ha. Oh, Rolfe does so love to dig, doesn't he? This whole thing might have been covered up." Miss

270

Tempie put her hand over her mouth as she laughed at her own little joke. "Covered up." She slapped both hands on the table, "And now he has to conk you two over the head with his shovel and bury you here. He's so good with that shovel."

CHAPTER TWENTY-THREE

Malinda jumped up and flung the table on Miss Tempie, who rolled over in her chair, sputtering and clucking like an upset hen. China broke in a clatter and silver clanged as it hit the flagstone floor. I grabbed the silver teapot and Malinda snatched up a huge footed tray. My hat fell off as we ran. We ran like our lives depended on it.

We ran past the swimming pool, turned into a garden and back the way we'd come. Or we thought it was the way we'd come. All the doors looked alike. We took the first unlocked door, shoving past massive furniture stacked to the ceiling and dark boxes big as refrigerators. *"Oof."* Malinda bumped into one as we rounded a corner. "The damn thing didn't move an inch." She stopped to rub her shoulder.

Fast behind her I said, "Look." The hall ended in stairs that curved up and a door that went down. The door had a padlock big and heavy as a purse.

We took the stairs, running, still carrying the tray and teapot. "If we run into anyone," Malinda said, "you douse him, I'll whang him then we run like hell."

At the top of the stairs, we hesitated, then took the hall to the left, both of us seeing what looked like light at the end of it. We tried locked door after locked door until we reached an open one, stood in the doorway and caught our breath. Verna lay asleep on the bed. At least she looked asleep . . . as Miss Lavinia had looked asleep. At first. Death was the ultimate deceiver. "You don't think . . . ?" I asked.

"She's sherried out," Malinda said. "Look."

I saw the mole on Verna's chin quiver as she suddenly sucked in a snore.

We went back the way we'd come, taking the other hall this time, the carpet so worn and dry it cracked like leaves under our feet. Dust rose and dried our throats, coated and filled our nostrils.

We turned the corner and saw more stairs. "I'm not going up any more," Malinda said, and we turned to go back, this time with me leading, only to find a heavy wardrobe blocking the way we'd come. "Damn, damn,

273

damn." I leaned against it, beat it with my fist.

"Maybe we can move it." Malinda grabbed an edge, pushed with her weight against it. Nothing moved. "It's solid as cement."

Somebody had moved the wardrobe, shut us in like cats in a cage. We'd die slowly here, clawing walls and screaming until we were too weak to breathe. No one would hear us. No one would come looking. Or if they did, not a thorough search. Miss Tempie would tell some half-witted tale like "the dear girls only stayed half an hour. So impolite, and young people these days have no time for manners and graciousness." Nobody would go looking through this monster of a house checking every hall and door.

"The stairs," I said. "There was a door at the top."

We ran down the hall again. This time we took the stairs to the third floor and ended up in a small room with a huge Palladian window arched like a church. "Lord," said Malinda, "I thought I'd never see daylight again."

There were double glass doors and we ran toward them and pulled.

"Stuck," I said. "Probably haven't been opened in fifty years."

"They're going to open now," Malinda said, and shoved her hip against them.

The doors stayed stuck.

"Hit it," I said, and with the teapot I started breaking glass.

Malinda hit it with her tray, fast and furious. The glass fell in front of us as we aimed blows and leaped backward, let the shards crash and splinter in jagged tears and deadly stalagmite crystals at our feet.

When most of one door had been cleared of glass, we broke the wooden frames and stepped onto a small, round porch.

"A damn balcony," Malinda said. "And I bet it's as rotten as the rest of the house." She put her hand out to hold me back. "It may be too much for both of us. Wait."

She eased to the rail and looked down. "If we crawl over, then drop, we'll be on the front porch with no broken bones."

Malinda hiked up her skirt and swung a leg over the rail.

I heard a muffled thump, the shifting of something large behind us. "Hurry," I said. "There's somebody in the hall."

Malinda was over the rail. From the balcony I heard a soft thump below, and Malinda said, "After you, Nancy Drew."

I grabbed the rail that wobbled in my hand and sent splinters prickling into my

275

fingers. I banged one knee, but I was over and hanging free by my hands. Then I let go and slid through cool air. I landed on my feet with a hard plunk that sent me off balance and rocking for a minute. But I was okay. Nothing broken, nothing damaged.

Malinda snatched me up beside her, close against the house. "He can't see us under here," she whispered. "When he goes back in, we run for the cars."

"But not on the gravel," I whispered. "Let's take it a cedar at a time." I pointed to the cedar spires, casting green-black pyramids of shadows beside the driveway. The shapes were large and would hide us quickly, completely.

Overhead we heard the boards in the balcony creak. Grit and filth rained down. Through the cracks, we saw soles of large shoes, heard the boards groan until the footsteps stopped at the rail, then give and groan again as he returned to the house. Only this time was another sound. A small sound that felt like glass at my chest. The clink of metal. A gun? Was Rolfe carrying a gun? Had it hit against the glass as he went though the door and back into the house? Or did he still carry that damn shovel and plan to hit us over the head before he buried

us in that "garden of earthly delights"?
"Run," I told Malinda. "Run faster."

CHAPTER TWENTY-FOUR

We made it to the first cedar, a tall, wide pyramid of deeper dark in the night shadows. There we paused a second and breathed hard before dashing to the next giant cone, then the third. We paused behind each cedar briefly and listened.

"Fifty more to go," Malinda said, and sprinted on with me behind.

That was when I thought I heard a shot. Something cracked in the dark. Then silence.

We zigzagged from cedar to cedar now and didn't pause. I could barely make out Malinda in front of me, and once Malinda stepped on a limb and said, "Damn," under her breath. My legs felt wobbly, and weak, as though they'd melt under me. I'd fall, have to crawl. But I'd do it if I had to. Crawl on my hands and knees to get away from this place.

Weeds and briars beat at my legs and I

stepped into a wild rabbit's nest. The rabbit let out a surprised squeal that sliced the silence and scared me so I started shaking. I felt hot and cold at the same time. My chest felt huge, hollow as a balloon. Yet I ran.

The end of the road didn't seem to be anywhere in sight. But it had to be close. We had been running continually downhill. The backs of my legs ached. They felt knotted and tight, being pulled tighter. I'd get a cramp and go down if we didn't get to the cars soon.

Almost as if Malinda read my mind, she called back, "There. We're almost there!"

I saw the spiked iron of the gates. The gates were still open, thank God, and beyond them waited the cars, safety and escape. Cramp or no cramp, I could crawl the rest of the way if I had to.

We were going to make it.

I heard Malinda's footsteps hit the road first, soft thuds, steady . . . getting there. Getting away.

I climbed the ditch and started around my own car when I ran into someone solid as a brick wall. "Ummpf," I said, then almost screamed, except the body started to feel warm and familiar and comforting. "Scott. Oh, Scott."

"Get in the truck," he said. "Quick." He hugged me for a moment, then held me around the waist and nudged me forward toward the truck door.

"But . . . Malinda, where's Malinda?" I grabbed the cool metal of the door handle.

"In," Scott said. "Now. She'll meet us back at the house."

He turned and headed out the way we'd come.

Scott drove the quiet streets where old trees made sinister shapes around the streetlights. I hugged myself and shook. I couldn't stop shaking.

Scott pulled me close. He drove with one hand, rubbed my arm with the other. "You're all right." He felt so warm and I felt so safe.

I nodded, then realized he couldn't see me. I said, "Just scared." The truck felt good, so good, like salt and skin and a sweetness from leather and oiled tools. I sighed and leaned back.

"Relax," he said, and turned the corner.

In the houses we passed, I saw lighted rooms that looked so ordinary. Comfortable. Safe. Houses that sat in the middle of green yards and looked quiet and normal. Normal, ordinary; good people going about their lives.

I hated Miss Tempie and Rolfe, for the evil they lived in. The ugly evil that had killed Lavinia Lovingood, Father Roderick and had tried to kill me.

Malinda waited at the curb in her Jeep in front of the Dixie Dew while Scott parked in back.

"So what do we do now?" She stood in the drive.

"We get some of Miss Margaret Alice's blackberry wine in us and pull ourselves together." He held the door for me and kept his arm around me up the steps and into the hall. I hadn't even locked my own door. Old habits die hard, or had I locked it and someone had unlocked it?

Scott steered me toward a wing chair and went into the dining room. Malinda took the sofa and dropped hard like something with weight had been suddenly let go. She sank into it, leaned back her head and closed her eyes.

I heard Scott open the sideboard. There was a thunk of bottles and then glasses clinking on a tray.

"When you guys didn't get back" — he came into the room — "I unlocked the house and waited inside. It started to get dark and I decided your tea party must have included something more unexpected."

He set the tray on a low table in front of us, poured three glasses, handed one to Malinda and one to me.

Malinda took a deep swallow, the wine staining her lips dark as ink. "Lord, that's good. Heat it up and I'll drink a quart, curl up here on this sofa and not go home till next week."

"You're not going home tonight, anyway," I said. "He's still out there and he may have a gun."

"Gun?" Scott asked. "Who?"

"Rolfe," I said. "Miss Tempie's hired man, hired gun and number one killer. I *thought* I heard a shot as we ran. I heard metal hit glass. But I was so scared I could have heard anything. Limbs breaking, twigs cracking."

"Back up," Scott said. He finished his cordial, poured another and refilled Malinda's and my glass, too. "Tell me from the beginning."

Malinda took off her shoes and rubbed her feet. Her skirt was torn and she had scratches on her arms and legs. Her hair looked tangled and wild.

My skin stung from scratches, but I didn't care. It felt too good to be home. Here with Scott and Malinda, having a normal conversation. Except it wasn't normal. It was about a murder. Or two. Or three?

"Miss Tempie killed Miss Lavinia," I said. "She and Verna sat at the table talking about it like last week's bingo game."

"It was absolutely unreal," Malinda said. "Hard to believe. Those two little old ladies . . . killers."

"Like something out of *Alice in Wonderland,*" I said. "The two queens battling back and forth and Miss Tempie lecturing on manners, pouring this god-awful tea."

"Yik," Malinda said, and poured more blackberry wine. "And Rolfe was the one who shut Beth into the mausoleum."

"His hand," I said. "His hand was bandaged. The one I cut with the X-ACTO knife."

"Sounds like Ossie DelGardo needs to pick up some people," Scott said. "That's the least he can do. You two have done the rest of the work for him."

Scott left to call Ossie. "He's probably in bed, but I don't think this ought to go on a minute longer."

"And whose bed might he be in?" Malinda started to giggle and couldn't stop. She bent in the middle, shook her head and laughed.

I laughed, too. The idea of the portly, saintly, sanctimonious Ossie DelGardo jostled from a tryst was too much. "You know something you haven't told?" I asked.

"Juanita." Malinda wiped her eyes and lay back limp on the sofa. "He was always checking her locks."

"Sure he was," I said. "Just doing his duty."

"Overtime," Malinda said, and started laughing all over again. "She makes his lunch on a hot plate in her upstairs apartment."

"Oyster stew," I howled.

"Only in the *r* months." Malinda screamed with laughter. "Won't get any next month, will he? Maybe we better leave town, not have to be around with all his nastiness. Bet you been thinking he was just born naturally mean. We don't know the half of it."

"Okay." Scott returned from the hall. "I couldn't get Ossie, but I got Bruce and he said what you two got would have to be considered hearsay evidence. He said he can't go around arresting somebody just because somebody *said* they murdered somebody. He'll consider Miss Tempie and Rolfe persons of interest and bring them in tomorrow morning, question them, get everything on tape, nice and legal. Meanwhile, he wants you two to mind your own business." Scott sighed. "And quit bothering the trained 'professionals' in this town."

"Trained professionals! My ass. Underneath he's really implying who is going to believe a woman crazy enough to start a bread-and-breakfast in a little Podunk town and a pharmacist who trips and falls in slime pits." I was mad. Mad at myself for even going to Tempie's tea. Mad at getting involved. Why did I ever think I could come home again? Could anybody, ever?

"Didn't trip," Malinda said. "And who told him? Barbershop gab. Blah."

"That's Bruce with his hip holster for you," I said. "And his billy."

"He's always got his billy. It's mono-grammed." Malinda slapped the arm of the sofa. "Carved with snakes to scare the bad guys away."

"Miss Tempie will go peacefully," I said. "But they'll have to wait while she packs her cosmetics bag."

"Then they'll be waiting until next week," Malinda said. "If she puts on her makeup. Oh, that woman and her vanity. Poor old thing."

"Poor old thing had us next on her little death list," I said, suddenly sober. "And she was checking us off."

"I called your mama." Scott turned to Malinda. "Told her you were staying here overnight."

"Thanks!" Malinda called back from the

hall where she was headed toward the bathroom. "You can make up my bed."

"There's four empty bedrooms upstairs!" I called. "Take your pick!"

"Three," Scott said. "Rupert Murchison came."

"Oh." I cupped my hands over my mouth. "I forgot all about him."

"No problem. I was here when he came. I signed him in and so on."

"I'm sacking out on this sofa." Malinda came back yawning. "Right there." She pointed. "It's me, my pillow and Miss Margaret Alice's granny afghan." She stretched her arms toward the ceiling and yawned. "Go. You two are keeping me awake."

"And you've had a haaard day," I said. "You mean running for your life just wears you out?"

"I'd rather be worn-out than laid out." Malinda wiggled her toes, pulled the afghan around her shoulders and curled into the sofa. "Good night."

I started to get the tray and glasses, but Scott motioned to leave it, come on. Malinda was already asleep.

"I don't think I can go to sleep that easily," I said.

"Take a hot bath," Scott said. "I'll check your locks."

I gave a half giggle. "You and Ossie Del-Gardo."

"What?" Scott said. "I missed something."

"Never mind," I said.

Later in the tub I felt myself smiling. Ossie and Juanita. Funny. I was glad I could laugh about something; that I could be that relaxed. The last few weeks had been tense and unreal, and if I were reading this in a book I wouldn't believe it. But all this had happened in my little town. I stretched, splashed and unwound, then lay back, closed my eyes and felt myself getting drowsy. The water had cooled, so I ran more hot water and soaked, letting every bad moment of the afternoon slough off. The whole nightmare of me and Malinda running through that decayed castle of a house with that henchman after us, then the drop from the balcony and the mad chase down the driveway with him right behind us. I slid deeper in the soothing water. I was relaxed now.

I was in bed with my light off when Scott cracked my door and leaned his head in. "Sleep well," he said.

"Wait," I said quickly. "Wait."

"Good night." Scott had one hand on the doorknob.

"Don't go."

"Even upstairs?"

"Here." I sat up, pulled back the sheet and slid over. "Sleep here."

"Are you sure?"

"Very sure."

He eased off his jeans and started to unbutton his shirt when he stopped and said suddenly, "I'll be right back." He shot out the door wearing a shirt, shorts and socks. Red socks. Were they warning flags? Where was he going and what had he heard?

In a few minutes he was back, under the sheet next to me, kissing me and more. I felt as if he'd always been right there. So right.

He kissed the back of my neck and moved down to nuzzle my shoulder.

"Oh God," I said.

"Yes," he answered, his breath warm and moist on my breast.

I pulled him close, closer, until his breath was my breath, his chest my chest, and then he was me.

"Oh my," I said suddenly. "Oh my goodness."

"Yes." He nibbled my ear. "Goodness gracious yes."

CHAPTER TWENTY-FIVE

I woke to the smell of fresh coffee, surprised I had slept. But it had been such delicious sleep. Except it wasn't the sleep. It was the sex and Scott. God, it had been so long. Too long. And now what? Where did that leave me?

When I reached for my robe, my arms felt stiff, as if I'd been stretched somewhere yesterday. I'd been stretched all right. Mentally and physically. My arms when I hung from Miss Tempie's balcony. My legs running up those stairs and frantically down the driveway that seemed ten miles long. Not to mention ducking from what I *thought* was a bullet, and all the tension during those hours of tea and confession with that henchman digging and shoveling, then standing guard outside the door.

And then there was Scott. Last night. I patted the empty bed beside me, pressed my face into his pillow. It still smelled slightly of a hint of his aftershave and something more. Something that made me stretch deliciously.

I wanted to stay in bed all day. I wanted to roll in these sheets and swaddle myself in them. Telling myself if I did, Scott would come back and find me and we would begin again where we left off last night. We would repeat and repeat until we were marvelously spent, until we fell exhausted off each other and the bed and began again on the floor. God, he was good. God, I was good.

The question was, Where was Scott now? The house was quiet. And what time was it?

I slid into my slippers and shook myself, combed my hair with my fingers. Where was Scott? Had I dreamed the whole wonderful thing?

I was tying my robe when someone tapped lightly on my door, then opened it.

Ida Plum stepped in carrying a tray, coffee and muffins. "Are you ready for this?" She motioned me back in bed. "Once won't spoil you, I don't guess."

I didn't protest but popped back in bed, plumped up my pillows and settled back, disappointed down to my toes that Ida Plum's head had appeared behind that tray and not Scott's. Where was he? This wasn't the way I wanted my first morning after. I always thought, after making love, I'd be the one to wake early and lie there watching someone else sleep. Possessing rather than being possessed. Hanging on to that wonderful feeling as long as possible. But, my God, he'd disappeared.

I couldn't let Ida Plum, bless her thoughtfulness, see how disappointed I was.

I sipped. God, he made good coffee.

"Malinda made the coffee," Ida Plum said.

If she was reading my mind, then I was embarrassed.

"I found it when I came in. With this note."

I read the note scribbled on a Dixie Dew B and B notepad: "If you need me I'm pushing pills. What a night. M."

"Her handwriting's as bad as a doctor's," I said.

"She almost was." Ida Plum poured herself a cup. "Remember? She was going into medicine. All that hoopla with the Morehead scholarship and her being black and female. Double token, they had, but none of the papers spelled it out that way at least."

"What happened?"

"I've never heard all of it. Or maybe even most of it. Or maybe not the truth of it. Rosalie never has been one to talk her troubles. One day Malinda's back, working at Gaddy's, degree in pharmacy and a baby. I never asked questions. Figured if Rosalie or Malinda wanted me to know something, they'd tell me."

"I've never asked either," I said.

"I'm just glad she was with you last night," Ida Plum said.

"If she hadn't been with me last night, I wouldn't have been where I was. I'm no match for Miss Tempie, handyman or not."

"Speaking of Tempie. Ossie called. He'll be by later to get a statement from you. He's talked to Malinda. He thought you'd like to know they charged Rolfe with Lavinia's murder."

"Father Roderick's, too?"

"Just killing Miss Lavinia. Rolfe also got charged with attempts on your life. And Tempie as accessory."

"Somehow I can't see Miss Tempie in a cell."

"Neither could Ossie, apparently. That's why he didn't take her in. She must have pulled her poor, pitiful Tempie act. She is a master at it. Years of practice."

"He let her go?"

"Until the trial. She confessed it was all her idea. She's good at confessing and he's got it on tape. He figured she wasn't going anywhere and she wasn't a threat to anybody." Ida Plum picked up my towel from last night. I almost worried Scott's blue plaid boxer shorts might drop out. Where were they? Where was he?

"Did he get the whole story?" I wanted to hurry and finish my coffee and get dressed, find out what was going on in the real world.

"Tempie had been embezzling from the church. They've had priests come and go. She's always done the bookkeeping and it was always sloppy. Nobody thought to check and recheck until Father Roderick came along."

I stopped with an orange cranberry muffin halfway to my mouth. "Our Miss Tempie? The quintessential little old lady?"

"Nobody but." Ida Plum opened the curtains and raised the window.

"And there she was giving me a lecture on manners and morals."

"Evidently she did it over the years. That's manners for you. A nibble at a time."

"Why?"

"She was accustomed to a certain lifestyle. You saw her house. It takes something to keep a house like that standing . . . even if it's not standing very well. Taxes go up every year, even on unoccupied property. And to keep her in cat food. It may be cheaper than tuna, but it still takes a couple of cans a week for casseroles and salad."

I loaded my knife with strawberry jelly. "I thought she taught music."

"She hadn't taught in years," said Ida Plum. "She had gotten to the place where she screamed at the kids relentlessly. Or that's what I heard. And more. It doesn't take corporal punishment to get a kid to practice music. Or it shouldn't."

"Probably did more than just whack their fingers with a ruler. She had a vicious temper." I shuddered, remembering how I had cowered under the fear of Miss Tempie's upraised hand holding that ruler like a guillotine ready to come down on my helpless fingers. "Where does Miss Lavinia fit into the picture?"

"According to Ossie, who, contrary to what you heard, has not been spending all his time with Juanita but digging through a lot of information and checking out sources, Lavinia was leaving everything to St. Ann's. That's where Father Roderick came on the scene. Doesn't surprise me a whit." Ida Plum sniffed. "He never struck me as the priest type. I thought he was too good looking."

"That's why she came back," I said.

"She was eighty plus. She knew she couldn't have a lot of years left." Ida Plum fluffed the curtains and wiped a finger of dust from my bureau. "I told you that from the first day you got her reservation. She wanted to be buried here. She just didn't plan on being buried here quite so soon. She planned to spend her last days in one of those new condominiums the church is building. She'd be taken care of until her last breath; then the church would take over from there with what was left of her money. And there was supposed to be quite a bit left. Or that's what I heard."

"And with all the inheritance, Miss Tempie's minor indiscretions over the years would be forgiven. Especially since she was the one who recruited and reunited Miss Lavinia with St. Ann's."

"Tempie just hurried up the process. At her age you get impatient." Ida Plum had her hand on the doorknob.

"And Father Roderick's housekeeper?"

"She killed Father Roderick. That all came out when Ossie talked to Tempie. Tempie knew it from the start. She just didn't tell. She always was one to keep things to herself. Thought she was too good to even talk to most people."

"Sounds like a domino effect."

"And both Tempie and Father Roderick knew the housekeeper stole Miss Lavinia's jewelry."

"Which Crazy Reba then stole from her when she went in the rectory to take a bath." Oh, it was all falling into place, domino after domino.

"When Father Roderick was going to report his housekeeper to Ossie DelGardo, he made the mistake of praying first. That's when the housekeeper strangled him." Ida Plum snorted. "His religion did him in. Maybe he was a real one. I just thought he did more playing at it than actual work."

"So it must have been Miss Lavinia's silk teddy. The housekeeper must have taken it when she stole the jewelry. The poor woman. She couldn't have fitted half her ass into it." I laughed. "It's all so curious."

"That's Littleboro for you." Ida Plum started out.

"But where do I come in all this?" I asked. "All I did was find Miss Lavinia and Father Roderick. And maybe get myself and Malinda half-killed. I didn't know anything or anyone who might have been in the murdering business."

There was no answer. Ida Plum had shut the door. By the time I got dressed and into the kitchen, Ida Plum was gone. She'd left a note. It was a day for notes, I thought, reading it. Ida Plum had written on a grocery shopping pad, below "Carrots" and "Bath-room cleanser:" "Your Mr. Murchison is still in bed. I did not take him a tray. One was enough and I'm not starting that. Hope he is not a repeat of Miss Lavinia. One was enough of that, too. I.P.D." Scott would laugh at those initials. The Ida Pineapple Department.

I forced myself up the stairs. There was only silence at the top. I waited outside Mr. Murchison's door. It was so quiet. I tapped on the door. Then tapped again. Please, not again. Surely, it couldn't happen twice. I'd be out of business fast.

I tapped again, leaned against the door and listened. Nothing moved. No one coughed or turned over in bed, or made a human sound.

I turned the knob and again waited. Nothing.

And nothing met me inside the room. Nothing and nobody. It was cleared out. There was a note on the dresser. "Left at 5 a.m. Thanks for a good night. Rupert Murchison." The handwriting was small, little mouse tracks across the page and as tidy as an accountant.

The bed was unmade, but the spread had been pulled up to neaten it and there were damp towels over the rod in the shower. Mr.

Murchison had been here and gone. Gone on his way and not to his reward. I was relieved. Oh, was I relieved. I didn't realize I'd been holding my breath until I sighed and started removing the sheets.

Sherman came in, hopped on the dresser and looked out into the maple whose leaves were unfolding at a fast rate. He looked as if he were thinking, Bird for lunch, bird for lunch. He flexed a paw against the screen, got it caught and began to pull.

"Trying to tear the house down, Sherm?" Scott poked his head around the corner. "The House of McKenzie stands on strong turf, old buddy." Scott pried the cat's claws loose, then picked him up and held him next to his chest.

"I just had a scare." I smoothed on fresh sheets. "When Mr. Murchison hadn't come down, I came up and it was the Monday morning of Miss Lavinia all over again. No answer when I knocked. Not a sound of someone in here . . . someone alive, that is. Then I opened the door and it was empty as a tomb."

"Unless it's a tomb that belongs to a Merritt." Scott put the cat down and helped me tuck in the sheets. I liked a guy who could make a bed. Or who didn't feel it beneath him to help make a bed.

I didn't like remembering the Merritt tomb. Sometimes, if I let myself, I could still smell that dry air, dust and darkness. Total darkness had a smell. I'd never forget that smell.

"Did you know when he left?" I wanted to ask a lot of questions, but that seemed the only safe question to start.

"I heard him," Scott said, "when he left, and earlier. He's a sleepwalker. That noise I heard last night just before . . . when I got up so suddenly . . . was Mr. M. standing at the top of the stairs in his skivvies, dead asleep."

I laughed. "He should have told us. Or locked himself in. What if he'd gone out the door? Walked down the street?"

"I got him all tucked in. Then he woke up and told me about leaving early, at five. I guess so I wouldn't come up and try to tuck him in again."

So that's where Scott went so abruptly last night. He never said and I hadn't asked. There had been too much to do. Too many new discoveries being made. "No more blackberry wine," I mumbled.

"What?" He picked up Mr. Murchison's sheets.

"Ida Plum told me about Ossie's call and Miss Tempie confessing. I still don't understand what it had to do with me."

"You were a threat to Tempie. And she was running scared. You came back to restore your grandmother's old house, turn it into a business."

"I can't understand how that was a threat to Miss Tempie. What it had to do with anything."

"Miss Tempie talked about that, too."

"She must have talked a lot," I said.

"She had a lot to talk about." Scott smoothed the bedsheets. "And Ossie listened well. You underestimate him."

"So who killed Mama Alice?"

"Nobody. She fell. That's what I'm saying. She simply fell down the stairs and never regained consciousness. It was a stroke that caused her to fall."

"But those notes Verna wrote?"

"Miss Tempie put her up to them. You knew that."

"Why?"

"To scare you off. To get you to give up the Dixie Dew and leave. Sell. In one word, that's what they wanted." Scott plumped a pillow, tossed it back on the bed.

"Sell to whom?" I asked.

"St. Ann . . . the diocese." Scott stood back to admire his plumping.

"The condominium project." I grabbed

the bundle of soiled sheets and damp towels to take downstairs. Maybe a laundry chute could be built up here to send this stuff downstairs in a fast slide. New project for Scott? "The Dixie Dew stands in the way, I guess. And you saw the architect's drawings, the blueprints?"

"A long time ago." Scott stood in the doorway, hands tucked in his pockets.

"That's why I had so much trouble getting workmen? Oh," I said, "it all makes sense now. And you were willing to help me."

"To save the Dixie Dew." He grinned.

"Is that the only reason?"

"One of them, and as good a one as any." He turned, went into the hall.

"About last night . . ." I started, but didn't get to finish. Scott had disappeared down the hall. I heard the vacuum roar, rattle and whine, thought there's something totally endearing about a man behind a vacuum cleaner.

The next edition of the *Littleboro Messenger* had the headline "Local Crime Solved," with a picture of Rolfe beneath, who was being held. "They made Rolfe look like the country's number-one threat to society." Malinda had brought in the newspaper and stood beside me at the kitchen counter reading over my shoulder. Farther down the page was "Local Native Found Dead" and a picture of Miss Tempie from when she graduated from Juilliard. Her body had been found in a wooded area on her vast estate, the article read. There was no evidence of foul play, and none was suspected. Miss Tempie was shown in profile. She was twenty-two, an all-American girl with a blond pageboy, beatific and wearing a single strand of pearls. She looked absolutely beautiful, ready to have the world worshiping at her feet.

"Suicide?" I asked.

"The slime pit." Malinda shivered. "Maybe her mother didn't tell her a lady never takes her own life. The coroner said she was dressed in white from head to foot. They even found a large white hat floating beside her."

"My hat," I said. Somehow it must have fallen off when I jumped up from that tea table. I hadn't missed it. "Lord, she must have looked like a water lily," I said, "against the black water. Monet would never have been inspired. Or some Pre-Raphaelite gone bad."

The third item on the front page read: "Evidence in Murder Case Still Missing." Miss Lavinia's jewels, reported to be worth a small fortune, still had not been recovered.

"I think you better turn yourself in . . . jewel thief," Malinda said.

"I forgot!" I said. "How could I have forgotten?"

"Think our local law enforcement will buy your story? Crazy Reba won't be a reliable source . . . even if she confesses to the original theft." Malinda flapped the sports section of the paper back and forth.

"I think as soon as the Mr. Green Polyester Pants Cousin gets his loot he'll be gone within the hour. No questions asked." I fixed Malinda a glass of iced tea. "Want a sprig of mint in it?" I asked. "Or parsley?"

"I never want to see another sprig of parsley in my life," said Malinda. "In fact, I almost break out in a rash when I hear the word."

I guess Miss Lavinia had been trying to write in her farewell note something about how it wasn't parsley. Or "That is hemlock" or "That is the last time I have tea with Tempie Merritt." I would never know.

Malinda and I spread the newspaper on the counter between us and read bits aloud.

"I really don't think our Ossie, as you call him, will question anything as long as he gets the rocks back."

Malinda turned the page to "Society

News," which I always thought was an oxymoron if there ever was one. "Look," she said.

"Engagement Announced." There was Ossie in full uniform, badge shining like a prize medal, his arm around Juanita with her two-level teased hair. He wore a fat-cat grin and Juanita's blinding white smile was as tight as her last face-lift and new set of dental implants would allow.

"Well, what do you know!" I said.

"Her third." Ida Plum came through with a set of sheets fresh from the ironer. "And who knows which it is for him."

"Going to the wedding?" Malinda asked.

"Maybe," I said. "I already know what I'm buying for a wedding gift."

Malinda shook her head, hand on the back door, heading out. "Aren't you suddenly the benevolent one!"

"A set of knives," I said. "And depending on my mood from now until then, I may or may not decide to enclose a coin to cut the bad luck."

Malinda left laughing.

I could truly wish both Ossie and Juanita happiness. And a long life. Longer than Miss Lavinia, Father Roderick and Miss Tempie, too, wherever her little soul had flitted to.

On the back page of *The Mess* was a reprint of an article that had appeared in the *Baltimore Sun* travel section: "Yankees Going South, Go to the Dixie Dew." The byline was of a Dillon Lucas, who must have been my mystery guest/travel writer who had spied on me and taken the photo of the Dixie Dew printed with the article. In the picture on the walk in front of the Dixie Dew was a woman strolling a big white rabbit on a leash. The rabbit seemed to be smiling as if he'd just eaten something green and delicious. The woman looked like she owned the street, the sidewalk, the world.

If you looked closely at the photo you could see someone sitting on the front porch in the swing, wearing a bulky blanket and enough jewelry to almost be considered a breastplate. She seemed to be singing and had her arms raised toward Heaven.

Happy is as happy decides to be, I thought.

All was well in Littleboro. The rest of the world I couldn't worry about.

The doorbell still rang, and I picked up Sherman on the way to the front door. The Dixie Dew was still in business.

Maybe.

ACKNOWLEDGMENTS

This is not to thank the members of my long-ago Charlotte writers' group who disliked this manuscript from word one.

My husband, who said "Whatever you do, don't write a novel. It takes too long. You'll never get it published and you can't plot."

My sons, who asked, "What do you know about running a bed and breakfast?"

Note to my academic cell mates: *Doing It at the Dixie Dew* has the only two subjects W. B. Yeats said were worth writing about: sex and death. Plus the third one: food.

Seriously: I *do* want to thank my good friends Mignon Ballard and Molly Weston, who eat, sleep, and breathe mysteries. A trillion thanks to Jane Dunlap, who is my computer guru and best buddy. Judith Stanton, who alternately calmed and cheered. The Saturday group at Joyce Allen's. Also, more thanks to Karen Pullen and Sisters in Crime. Plus the Writers'

Police Academy. Cathey Kidd — and she knows why. And more thanks than anyone can imagine to my genius editor, Toni Kirkpatrick, whose talented pen made this a better book in every way.